Moments in Bougainville
A Collection of Short Stories

Leonard Fong Roka

DEDICATION

To the many Bougainvilleans who had, in one way or the other, an influence on my life before, through and after the Bougainville crisis and especially, those in the mountainous village of Kupe, those in Arawa and those in the Tumpusiong Valley in Central Bougainville. Also to my late father, John Roka, from Bali Island, West New Britain Province - sadly you are not here to read what I write.

CONTENTS

ACKNOWLEDGMENTS

Thanks to Pukpuk Publishers and Phil Fitzpatrick for his time to groom this work and words of encouragement offered since 2011.

Also to the blog, "Keith Jackson & Friends: PNG Attitude". Writing for the blog and taking part in the "Crocodile Prize", Papua New Guinea's national literary competition founded by Phil and Keith in 2011, has helped me develop as a writer. And to my lover and partner, Delpine Piruke for her love and care when I needed it most.

Lastly, my thanks to you, the one who is reading this book.

1
THE BLOODY FRONTIER

"No class today, boys and girls," Miss Ketu, a year five student, interrupted the silent community of her classmates as she dashed for her desk. Carelessly, she raked her scattered books and biros and packed them into a nicely designed Papua New Guinean highlands *bilum*.

The class was disturbed and mentally dispersed like a pack of sleeping wild bats. Was this related to this month's Papua New Guinea gun-boat gunning off the coast, a few wondered?

"What is that girl doing?" a couple of contemptuous voices chorused as Miss Ketu rushed for the doorway. Their expected mid-term test was no more!

"Eh, Mrs Takinu has gone to Happy Valley to see her husband; he is leaving for the Solomons this afternoon – or tonight."

Silence enveloped the class as the messenger left.

This was Bougainville in 1991 and Mrs Takinu was a math teacher at Bovo Community School in Arawa. She was a newlywed and expectant mama.

Five months pregnant; she was a proud mother to be. Often she boasted about what a nice baby she would be cuddling soon.

In the school her good temperament and attitude towards the students earned her high levels of respect compared to the rest of the staff. Lately, however, her class was often bored with her continuous complaints about headaches.

Her husband, Mr Takinu was also a fine citizen of the suffering township that had been swiftly turned into a sort of a military camp.

He had broad shoulders, light fuzzy-wuzzy hair and the

slightly thick lips that Kietas often referred to as 'African Lips'.

Because of his sex jokes he was considered by the students to be a sex maniac…a soul that can't go without a bit of it for the long restive night. Across their Namira Street, opposite Bovo School, this was the topic of the moment. The couple was often spotted kissing on their veranda, like Europeans.

Upon arrival at Happy Valley, in the former port township of Kieta, Mrs Takinu noted that a sixteen foot outboard motorboat was already geared up ready for departure. Her heart shook in her chest. What was provided for her husband? The child?

But before her the dingy danced to the rhythm of the waves as if answering her doubts. It was equipped with four hundred litres of petrol, her staple food. And before her the crew were like bees sorting out this and that for the journey.

At the bow a few swollen travelling bags were piled up. Mr Takinu's bag was the obvious one; it was the newest, recently purchased from across the Solomons by a friend who had crossed over for medical treatment.

Four or five high powered rifles also had a place on board since they were the only means of hope across the bloody frontier. Many a soul without guns had fallen before them.

Her heart ached as she watched the men. Five of them were to venture out during the night hours amidst that scary expanse of the Solomon Sea. No wife caressing and sweet whispers in the heat of the night!

She felt a sharp spasm of pain in her left thigh and wondered what was going on. Thick clouds continued building up just below the roots of her curly hair and wouldn't let her think of anything more pleasant.

Amongst the men she watched the father of her child, laughing, excitedly aloof. Is this the last smile? She silently questioned all his actions.

Everything was tangled up in her upset mind. There was no one out there to sort them out. Here she stood with a child…and, here also was the papa leaving for a gloomy and dreadful mission.

"E, good day, woman." Someone approaching interrupted the peak of the storm.

As if surprised by an unseen object, she reluctantly replied: "E," And then remained silent since there was nothing else to pacify the mental turbulence she was struggling through.

Is this journey a pleasure trip she was wondering looking at the men who seemed to be unbothered by anything? This was male culture!

Bougainvillean men had died in that sea of foreign gunships that came from the northwest. What do they want here in the Solomon island of Bougainville? An encounter with those rusty floating hulls always meant death - sacrificing one's own life on an ocean administered by those blood-hungry sharks.

"Well, well missus Takinu…you seem depressed today," Onana, the skipper said.

Mrs. Takinu didn't respond quickly. She was surprised by what she saw! Long-time no see; and her kinsman, the skipper, had farmed himself a pot-belly and blossoming baldness. A few wrinkly lines were running across his face as well.

He was growing old faster than she thought. What is wrong with him? Maybe, the harmful impact of the tropical sun was upon his body? The whiteman's theory of rapid death of body cells couldn't be so for him?

Getting no answer, Onana sauntered on towards Takinu who was now resting against the trailer of his Toyota Hilux. His bulging brown eyes were fixed on the west side of unpopulated Pokpok Island. He was a tourist admiring the island that had recently been a target for the evil Papua New Guinean gunboats.

"E, your wife is stony today," Onana said with a laugh,

"what, you had a row and came anyway?" His eyes of mockery were on the woman.

Takinu was quick. "Oh, you know, the brewing storm, so play me no pranks. Your wife is my aunty, you know that, she would understand... but that is on the outside."

"E, I see - ," Onana was interrupted by the loud closing of the car door.

Mrs Takinu moved lazily towards them and positioned herself against her husband. Cautiously, Onana watched her.

"Aung, you see that?" she said, directing her glance at Onana. "That ocean, where thousands of years ago your ancestors crossed to colonize this beloved country of ours has no mercy for you today."

"E, I see that, my mama." Onana was swift and brave. "Have faith in the Lord, for our struggle and death is for the good of the land he has given us."

"You are right, but that God, they say - people say - works to no avail these days. He sleeps, maybe in Jerusalem, as we die for our beloved island."

"E, your bad mind," Onana chuckled, hopelessly.

"Yes man," she said, sharply, "you cry but he is snoring somewhere in the clouds."

Onana was defeated by the sharpness of her educated brain. To him, consoling her would be like banging his head against a brick wall; it was not worth marching into one's own grave. Let her suffer in her private shell.

Takinu was disturbed by his wife's attitude to Onana. He didn't want to be travelling with a perturbed voyage partner. Maybe, when his wife was out of sight, he would turn to placate him. But at least, he must utter a word for them. Should he? Yes.

With a serious expression he began: "E, my two friends, especially you my woman, know that where there is will; there is always a way out of that storm that is bothering you. We must not be the burden for our worry is that child in your womb, for his future is at stake from the infidel Papua New Guineans, my wife."

He was jubilant deep in his heart. His carefully selected words had attained their purpose; that is, to turn the argument the other way round: the woman must forget them because, every man whose wife does not freely let him do what he wants, in all aspects of Kieta life, is always a failure.

But she was still out of sorts with dark clouds sweeping her innermost world. She was lost in the midst of the tempestuous Solomon Sea. She was silent, lost between her husband and the child, who was not receiving the fatherly attention it required.

Onana felt like jumping up and down in victory for the support, but cautioned himself so as not to evoke more trouble with his kinswoman, who was obviously in pain right there under his big nose. So he kept quiet and calm as the sea before him.

It was very late in the afternoon as the shrilling of the insects diffused through the salty breeze over Kieta. Then the saddened expectant mother left with her brother for Arawa. Warm tears rolled freely down her chocolate cheeks as she took a last glance at the southern Kieta sea passage from Premier Hill in the rear view mirror.

The Bougainville Revolutionary Amy and civilian boats crossing to the Solomon Islands for humanitarian needs used the passage most of the time for quick access to the open sea. Ahead the setting sun was already behind the Ovoring Boulder that stands so high on the Crown Prince Range. It is a giant in its own right, looking west from Arawa, she is always there.

To the north, white seagulls were above and about the Loloho port bay area. Just below her, in the Kobuang Bay village a shoal of dolphins were parading in harmony on their way towards the open sea. Why don't the enemy Redskins hunt you my fellow brothers of the sea? She felt jealous of nature but somehow it relieved the burning agony. "Come back, my love," she said to herself.

11

Back in the ghostly death town of Kieta the men sat like statues waiting for the hour. Darkness blanketed them and made them feel braver to endure what lay in wait for them. The cool salty sea breeze calmed them further. God was on their side, they knew that.

The hours dragged by in fine fashion, as all true Bougainvilleans know, and ticked over to the long awaited moment.

"Men, the hour they said we are to take off, is here," shouted Kauona, excitedly. "Where is the skipper or I'll take over."

"E, Kauona you keep quiet. I know you just want us to hurry up, so you can see those girls in Gizo," Ruru called out with a laugh, as he lazily massaged his M16 A2 rifle. "You call yourself a BRA commander but are spoiled by a little girl out there."

"E, not me only. You are the worst. Here you tell the people that you are going to shop for ammunition but there, you are shopping for a certain kind of bullet in the hotel rooms."

There was a roar of laughter and they all contributed their exaggerated comments on either side. All also knew that Kauona had a Shortland Island girl pregnant and his going was for no return because he loved the girl too much. His crossings into Bougainville had been intermittent but regular and mostly for the Bougainville Revolutionary Army.

Crossing the sea passage regularly, meant that this slim and unkempt man had more experience than anyone else aboard of the dangers of the unpredictable. He had fought and survived numerous gun fights and gunship attacks. He knew how the atmosphere smelled just before an encounter with the enemy, he knew that for sure.

"Well, Onana says we are taking off in thirty minutes time to see your good girl," interrupted Takinu, as he climbed into the dingy carefully so as not to fall off balance.

Onana returned to the boat after peeing behind the huge rain trees that stood along the seafront like lazy warriors ready to die at any moment.

His brown eyes carefully studied all the men, just like any teacher in a classroom would do if they were the type to enforce tidiness and neatness among the pupils. All the men were now on board, ready to break the blockade. One or two, were staring into the night sky, counting the twinkling stars. But all were ready for the journey.

Ruru, the youngest on board and Koimoi, were arguing in *Tok Pisin* about the exact location on the west coast of the lifeless Pokpok Isle they had wandered to for a dance a few months back. Tonight, however, there was no life. Foreign gunboats had scared away the people and they had fled to the motherland.

In the foreground a shoal of fish broke to the surface splattering water everywhere. Osiko, the oldest man bound for the Solomons was surprised and he gazed at the spot without blinking as the boat started its journey through the calm of the night.

In the blackness and in the little light generated by the distant stars the silhouetted landmass of Bougainville was speeding north as the boat headed bravely south.

In the distance Tausina Island, Pokpok's faithful sister islet emerged into view. A dark and exhausted oil tanker she was, after a long day's work.

The great landmass stood steadfast and waved goodbye to her children as they travelled south to visit their relatives.

The coast had no life, it seemed, but there is always someone out there in the night just like the brothers on the little boat.

There is always life but it must stay hidden for fear of falling to the lethal guns of the enemy or being inadvertently harmed by its own country fighters, for there are always men on the coastline with their guns defending the beloved nation in ruins; a nation that is owned by our dear mothers, who are now weeping in the jungles for their sons who die for loyalty to the land of their heritage.

Ruru stood in the bouncing bow with his PNGDF M16 rifle. His muscular body was heroic and alert, keeping the men informed of anything strange, like drifting logs, before them. Perfect he was as a navigator.

The men, though, were overwhelmed by the northward chill created by the speeding dingy. All except Takinu and the skipper who were intermittently exchanging words that Ruru could not hear properly because of the speed-created wind. The skipper's orders, however, were quickly decoded for the wind allowed just enough to reach his hairy ears.

"By the way, how many hours have we got to Taro?" Takinu asked loudly after a long silence. This was the first port-of-call for all Bougainvillean boats coming to the Solomons. "You've got a lot of experience, Onana, how many hours will it take?"

The skipper was unsure. He only vaguely knew about hours and minutes. He knew that when the long hand pointed at 12 and the short hand at the figure 8 it was eight o'clock, but nothing about time, distance and speed. So, his creative mind just gave out an estimate based on what he heard the others saying and by applying his own logic to the calculations.

"E, it's about five hours from Happy Valley to Taro with this 75 horsepower, boss." Whether, his guess was right or wrong, that didn't matter. He must be the man seen to be the master of where he travels.

The chill penetrated deeper into everyone's bone marrow and made them silent. But for Kauona, a strange feeling of loss was enveloping him. He tried to fight it off, but he couldn't. What wrong had he done in Arawa? Or, had he wronged the gods of the land? He searched and searched in silence and still he saw that the roads he had walked along were singing him farewell.

"Fuck yah, have we passed the Aropa BRA outpost, men?" Kauona shouted intentionally to help fight the creeping fear. That surprised the respected oldie, Osiko, whose grey haired head, heavy with sleep, had been swaying to and fro.

"Yes aung, we are just passing it," the skipper called out loudly. "But, you not respecting the chief, that's the one you ought to be looking up to as you grow older day by day."

Kauona glanced at the old bone and chuckled. "Very sorry, big man," he said, rubbing his eyes to get rid of the salt spray.

"Nothing to worry about," the aged one said, stretching his legs to balance himself more. "Just, take good care of us because the sea is becoming big tonight."

Ruru, the navigator enjoyed all these little commotions for they were exactly what he needed to keep awake and alert instead of succumbing to the swooping sleepiness of his eye lids.

"Talk men. Talk and we go on," he called out in a loud determined voice fighting the cold gusts of wind. He paused, then seeing one of his passengers, the elegant looking one, Koimoi who hailed from the Torauan village of Rorovana, but who was fluent in the Nasioi language added, "Have we some women that need to hide their fear of strangers by sleeping?"

Koimoi knew the sharp eyes of the navigator were on him. He was the one. Not a word had slipped out of his mouth between Kieta, right to this very point.

"E, stop gossiping and do the talking," he said, in an insolent voice but with a grin that exposed his areca nut stained teeth. Sleep was hard on him.

Behind them Kauona stood up unsteadily, as the boat bounced over a myriad of waves. Just like everyone else, he was fighting to prevail over the invading sleepiness of his eyes.

Seeing that no one else was interested in talking he began to stir up the air.

"I am a highlander from Kongara, you know but these

coastal girls turned me into a seafarer," he said reluctantly, facing Koimoi and Ruru. "What sort of love potion do you two think this Onana and his mothers have? You two don't back him," he added with a laugh and a tone desperate to keep the jokes going, "Onana ran after your salty mothers when they opened their legs to him in a way the Kongara women never do."

Peals of laughter broke from every man. Life was dawning like morning.

"Yes, Onana, that's salt power," added Koimoi, "when a salty coastal woman leaches you, you'll just forget Kongara forever."

The jokes carried them further towards freedom and away from the sting of sleep. Past the Aropa BRA outpost they went. They were right outside the Koromira area when Ruru spotted torches.

"Hey, there it is," Ruru interrupted, "that's Aropa, the BRA outpost. Am I right?"

Everyone came to life and looked at the place where they believed the BRA boats were stationed. They all concluded that someone on duty had just heard the motor and must be blinking his torch at them for fun, just like them, in his battle against the common enemy, sleep.

"See them, I just can't imagine how our boys cope with the long sleepless nights," Takinu said lazily.

"Just adaptation is all you need, along with the confidence the gun brings," an invigilate whisper came from Koimoi.

The lone torch bearer was now joined by another. Both men were some distance apart from each other, taking turns to torch-play on the boat people.

From the vast expanse and excluding the boat's speed or ability to reach the seashore Kauona worked out that the men were pointing south and then back at them. Was something wrong further south? But instinct, cried go on, 'don't be bothered, son.'

Were his friends on the boat working the same thing

out? In Kieta, there is a saying: 'The man who is most fear stricken will survive the ordeal.' He either went to war that way or did not go there at all, so he survived.

"Hey, they might be trying to tell us something," he said, his eyes fixed on the coast, "what do you think, should we go hear from them?"

"E, another waste of time, Takinu and Onana chorused. "Let go off that spirit of cowardice."

The words to respond against were far too many for him. He must fight on for he too needed to be there to see and be with his family.

Fear slowly crept up his spine. His heart trembled. In his sane mind, he envisaged death drifting in the dark sea. He felt like jumping overboard but calmed himself.

Humiliated he now got himself seated. He knew that something was wrong. But after sorting his mind out, he slowly moved to the front close to the navigator who was singing some Catholic Lenten songs. There he was safe; experience had told him so over the years.

Behind the two vigilant watchmen, storytelling and laughter broke out. What surprised most of the men was that the usually silent oldie, Osiko was in the heart of it all.

"Boys, this is the best trip I'd ever had. All the wise persons on board are making me want to cry, "Onana said, to Osiko's giggle. " Or what do you think, wise one?"

"Yes, the best," the oldie chuckled in the dark, "for the good health of the women down on the streets of Gizo."

"That's it," Takinu agreed. "For it is the setting sun that destroys; it cracks the earth and damages, you say Osiko, your old penis is not yet dead."

Leaving Aropa behind, the first forty litres of petrol was used up. The boat slowed and the fuel intake hose was transferred to the next container and the machine kept going with determination.

The night seemed harmless and at ease. High in the sky, bats were heading to the mainland to feed. In the space dominated by the twinkling stars, shooting stars rushed here and there.

Further out towards the open sea, enormous waves were crashing over the barrier reefs. How were those reef animals standing up to those forces of this great water, Kauona was wondering?

The lone boat was now in the Koromira waters. A place notable for its peaceful people as Kauona tells everyone when he travels there. Sometimes one hears him condemning himself for splitting up with his former girlfriend, who was from this district. Just the utter of the name, Teteomei, which is one of Koromira's huge boulders, makes him sick with imagination. Her love making had been of such prowess as to make him desperate to remain in bed forever.

"E, Osiko we are in Koromira south," Ruru shouted to the laughing men.

Osiko, the old one, was now the story teller. "In the 1930s while working in the Kekereka plantation, which today is your town of Arawa, I befriended a girl from here, that's in Koiano … "

"Why did you leave her?" someone interrupted him.

"Her stupid papa chased me with an axe." Exaggerated laughter broke out for his benefit.

The boat had just passed a pair of islands. Somewhere on the dark coastline was the Koromira Catholic mission. They all knew that; these islands were telling them.

"We'll make it to the Laluai delta before crossing into the open sea," Ruru told Kauona as they stood unsteadily against the regular bouncing and tilting motion of the dingy.

Kauona wiped the salty water from his face with his bare right hand and thought of all the debris the great river, Laluai brings to the sea.

"Aung, why not cross from here?" he asked the navigator.

"It's okay from here but the estuary area is better according to Onana. Brother, don't ask me for what reason for I have none in my mind." They laughed at their own ideas of the reasons.

Among the seated group, Koimoi seemed alive while the rest minded the things in their private worlds.

"Somewhere out there should be Koiano," he said to stir up the men to talk again.

"Yes, and you ought to be there," Takinu chimed in as he scooped seawater to rinse his mouth.

On their right appeared a group of desolate and vulnerable looking islands. They knew nothing about the world outside. Maintaining harmony with their surroundings was their fundamental concern.

"I wish I could settle there," Koimoi was telling Takinu, pointing at the islands.

"Tonight, I think. We'll settle," his friend said absent-mindedly.

The boat took a change of course. It altered its parallel run with the long barrier reef that runs all the way from Loloho and began to head into the open sea. In so doing, it smashed into a shoal of fish that suddenly took to the air and then fell back into the water.

In the darkness they could not spot the muddy Laluai estuary but the tiny islets ahead told them that this was the right area.

As Ruru directed, the boat zigzagged through the muddy water to avoid a few sparsely scattered drifting logs. At Kongara, the source of this great river, it was raining.

"E, Onana," Takinu cried, excitedly. "You are far too experienced."

"Salute Ruru," Onana added.

As the boat was fast approaching the last islet of the group Kauona felt a sudden gust of pain and extreme fear. Sweat freely covered his whole body. A sense of doom enveloped him. Were the others feeling the same? He guessed not because his mates were all still reacting like tourists. But his eyes were alert like all soldiers.

In an unstable voice he said: "Well, all our lives now

depend on you two - skipper and your navigator." To his dismay, Ruru just gave a gleeful laugh, like a carefree girl not bothered by any regulations.

But to their shock, the last islet was not a piece of land. It was the gunboat they had been trying to avoid at all costs. Waiting it was, for their blood. It was positioned perfectly against the silhouetted landscape of an islet like sisters gossiping.

From the distance the islet's shape well camouflaged the lethal PNG weapon from the poor Bougainvilleans. They had made it right into its arms like a child coming home to its father.

A blast went off! Old Osiko, made a thousand or so signs of the cross even though, he was a Protestant and hated Catholics. Ruru opened fire in the direction of the enemy.

Tears of defeat freely rolled down Kauona's cheeks as he waited for the secondary explosion of the flare in the night sky that would expose them to the barrel of the big gun.

The gunboat's awaited air-bound explosion went off. Mice in a cat's claw they had become. They were doomed! The burning flare above gave them a clear view of the boat. Magnesium was burning fast so another explosion followed.

Then came the heavy gunfire aimed at the tiny vessel that was now circling without a skipper in control because Onana was trying to control old Osiko who had nearly taken an early suicide into the sea. It's not worth killing oneself, before an enemy cools his rage on you.

"Lay flat in the boat, *pini*," Onana ordered Osiko as he handed Ruru an ammunition magazine.

"But my wife... my wife," the old man wailed in the storm of bullets. Onana left the old man to Koimoi and concentrated on the boat.

The armoured enemy never ceased fire and kept chasing its prey. It dearly wanted the blood of the black man. The Bougainvillean who had leached away the wealth needed to build his country; and now, all he wanted was 'no more black man' in the Pacific.

Kauona only fired semi-automatic rounds, taking careful aim at the machine-gunner who regularly took cover leaving the big weapon without an owner. The problem was he was not picking him off and there were many backups in that metal hut.

After firing two more shots as the enemy popped up he lay down and began fixing his weapon that had just jammed. Fumbling in his bag for possible tools he found none and had decided to sit idle when Ruru gave a hysterical scream.

Blood was visible on his thigh. He was squeezed into a corner like a cold child and remained there groaning. Kauona moved closer to take a good look of him; to his shock his friend was clamping his open palm over his belly trying to force his intestine into its rightful place.

"Don't bother about me brother," Ruru said in a quivering voice, "I'll fight to the last breath. This is our fight; this is our freedom, for Bougainville must be known."

The words gave them life. They were the last moment of hope for the men at the cross roads of death. It was better dying for Bougainville than dying in a hospital from AIDS.

Ruru picked up his weapon, with the barrel just 30 centimetres from Kauona's right ear, he began firing.

"Keep the fire cover!" Onana shouted at the navigator. Then he completed a u-turn and started heading towards the nearest islet in a zigzagging course.

But during this act of daring, the enemy intensified its fire power. The dingy was lost in the bullet-made geysers. The thudding sound of bullets hitting human flesh in the boat shocked Kauona.

Beside Takinu lay Koimoi who was raked through the ribs by the bullets. He was bleeding out his life slowly in agony.

But the chase got tougher. Above the flares dominated the sky, giving light to all - the hunter and the hunted. The wanted boat was just a naked girl subjected to the will of her aggressive boy. Bullets criss-crossed at will, and all one could do was just jerk or bend to avoid the red-hot metal of death coming at the speed of light.

To Kauona's surprise and desolation Onana screamed and went down into the water thrown by the force of a stray bullet. A forgotten boat anchor, the fine humorous skipper of skippers, he was. Pieces of his raked warm flesh stuck on his fellow comrades. He was gone, taken by war before their very eyes.

"We are finished, but Bougainville is not," someone wailed as the bullets hit the boat engine, halting it instantly.

Ruru lost all his might and kneeled and bent his head to the floor. "Brothers, if anyone is alive, go!" he cried in a smile of death. "Dive into the sea and go. Go to my mother and tell her: 'Shed no tears, for Ruru is free.'"

Nobody responded; though there was a mass of bodies no one knew for sure if they were alive or dead.

Kauona was startled when someone moved. The being splashed in the water building up inside the boat. It was Takinu, and he was still conscious.

"Go, brothers. Go home," Ruru gave call and landed in the water heavily. He did not move again.

The boat was now partially submerged as Takinu took off into the dark lifeless water; only to resurface a few meters away to be welcomed by a storm of bullets.

Kauona lay calculating his next step in tears. Above him burned three flare parachutes. The sight would seem enjoyable for the kids back home. The machine gunners halted fire and watched from the deck in a neat line. Is the mission accomplished?

Next to Kauona rested old Osiko in the blood stained water; his tongue protruding and the dead Ruru's bullet maimed left arm resting across his neck.

Kauona must swim through the water before the human enemy or the sharks arrived to scavenge. He picked up a loaded floating rifle. The flares above grew weaker and the gunboat men began to move about freely.

Out of the water he rose with defiance, finger on the trigger, and squeezed it and the bullets went off. One of the bastards landed in the water. As the magazine emptied, he shouted and sank into the water to swim beneath for what he hoped would be the length of a soccer pitch.

Through the water he went. A perfect frogman he was. Above him, bullets broke through the water, but below he went on.

The lone survivor resurfaced after several minutes. Was he to cry on water or on the land?

He was out of breath and vomited water. His legs were powerless but he managed to keep afloat as he gasped for oxygen.

A sense of fear engulfed him. Were the killers watching him? No, he shouldn't think that way, he must not come a cropper.

Behind him the patrol boat was in the vicinity of the dingy. Like brothers, they stood sharing jokes. A search light was on; as were the flares above. A few figures walked around doing this and that.

As Kauona's breath returned strength came back as if he was a long lost child returning home. He kept himself afloat. His legs paddled hard against the tide carefully watching all, the enemy's activities.

He had his eyes transfixed on the gunboat and wondered if all his fellow voyagers had died. "Is anyone out there?" he asked himself.

Something caught his attention. A helmeted sailor gesticulated followed by a deafening explosion in the water. There were jets of steam, as the detonation diffused. It was a hand grenade, a familiar sound.

So there was no hope. Gone were the boat people he had, just minutes ago, been laughing with. Death was a thief, as they say.

He began to submerge for the next swim but was interrupted by a new interest of the enemy as they fired rounds into another area of attention. The vessel steamed towards the target. Thank you for letting me go, you dirty dogs. But who is that other Bougainvillean?

The crew with guns crowded with interested gestures. It was the direction that the young father had taken. He recalled clearly now as he heard the cheerful shouts, swearing and cursing. Poor Takinu, but anyway your child is there to replace you.

Through the sea of blood, though, it was a lucky escape. The warm sun found him lying prone on the white sandy beach of June, one of the betraying islets. He was weeping.

High in the blue sky birds were not to be seen. They were weeping for a motherland that had just lost her children. The seagulls knew that in the afternoon it would rain cats and dogs to wash away the blood of the black men, so they too left for their havens.

Dedicated to Richard Kikila from Rorovana village, who was lost to the PNG gunboats in 1992 whilst crossing this line. Lest We Forget those Bougainvilleans.

Redskins - Bougainvillean term for Papua New Guineans.
Pini - Nasioi language; derogatory term for 'penis with a foreskin'.

2

FAREWELL MY BOUGAINVILLE PROPHETESS

The stench of body odour and sweat poisoned Dabuna's psyche as she jostled her way through the flesh of high spirited travellers in the Buka airport departure lounge. On her tail was her proud mama, Itonani, who braved her way through the curious eyes of the black men hanging onto the windows silently saying goodbye to their fellow countrymen and countrywomen.

Laborious was the posture of the queue for the check-in counter but the joy for a daughter going to the foreign land of *erereng* to be educated belongs not in the pocket. It was something to be expressed by being beside her daughter, steadfast till she was airborne.

Dabanu, the great woman of Kongara, secured her boarding pass with a dancing heart, for going away from her Bougainville in an air plane to study and become a teacher was a milestone. She hugged her grey haired mama and together they took an edge of a bench and sat.

"Dabanu, my daughter," she consoled her baby as they sat waiting for the big bird to land, "you are the light of those backward and barbaric mountains of Kongara. The Kieta people blame us for all the trouble that happens in Arawa; but it is us that saved their land from the cruel erereng that dug a big hole in the heart of our island with their big company, that thieving Bougainville Copper Limited".

"Kietas are like that, mama," Dabanu cried, as she got herself hunched ready in a corner near the boarding gate, "They think we are the scent of trouble in the land. But it was us who died to fight those ever thieving erereng that were colonizing our land and minds."

Out of no-where the plane roared as it landed upon the Bougainville soil. It taxied to a stunning halt to their north and, with a quavering roar again it entered the clear space before them. The pair watched in wonder as the airport men maneuvered to and fro, doing their jobs.

It was white and so imposing. Dabanu had a thorough look at it as people began to enter the terminal as swift as eagles. On it were the symbols - a Bird of Paradise and the words, 'Air Niugini' - of the distant country and people that had ruled their land since that fateful year, 1975.

"Mama, *si damaiko simenang*," her mama hugged her as tears rolled down her aging cheeks. "*Tampa sikuru darabaing*; Bougainville, the land your brothers and sisters died for needs you".

"Don't worry mama," Dabanu consoled, fighting off tears.

"My daughter," Itonani sobbed, "you are the future of your clan; you are the mother of the land of Tairima and you are the blood of Bougainville's future for which our people from Buka to Buin have died and suffered for under the terror of the cruel *erereng* since the days of the Germans.

"Be careful and never wander away from your school for the land of the *erereng* is a land of rapists, rascals, murderers and false gods - men of the street that preach till night. Yes, daughter you know it as the newspapers tell us who these people are. They did the same in our land so we had to fight and chase them away and now we enjoy our freedom on our island".

The mother and the daughter were still clinging to each other in the deep sorrow of losing each other. The other travellers began jostling through the exit for the plane that was waiting outside in the shimmering heat of the day.

"My daughter," the saddened mother, sobbed, "please remember those word of your uncle Birengka as he farewelled you at Kakusira. He said, 'As populations increase, our land is not expanding and this means land has a store of conflicts for you, Dabanu. So you have to marry a man who knows your myths and family history. This is a man from a clan our family has marital relations with since the dream times. My niece, this is your power to laugh off liars."

Itonani let go of her daughter and helped her with her handbag and tidied her tangled shirt at the collar.

"Remember your father," the sorrow shaken mother added as an afterthought, "he died for the good of our land and your future as a Bougainvillean on Bougainville and not a nobody. Love not an alien that does not know your myths and will not stand to support you when conflicts arise because he is stranger without roots in Bougainville or Choiseul where your progenitors come from."

Dabanu, with tears running freely down her cheeks, marched for the exit broken hearted. She was now leaving her beloved mother in tears, a sin she hated. The mother who had brought her up without a father because he had been killed by the *ererrng* army as he fought for their rights to be Bougainvilleans.

Her mother was her life. Her mother was all the reason for her existence through the war that the ererrng had fought so they could steal Bougainville's wealth and resources.

"Be educated my love, and come back and help Bougainville to be free." The last words of her beloved mother echoed in her head as she entered the plane.

Directed to a seat, she sat in tears looking out of the window. The plane rattled towards the runway and after a few seconds she was high in the sky like an eagle; but this was an eagle, she seemed to be comfortable with.

As the northern tip of Bougainville faded from sight, she was mesmerized by the beauty of Buka Island as it drifted below on the vast blue sea of Solomon. Her land was truly a paradise of black people.

Her flight was scheduled for a stop-over in Rabaul so

she kept her eyes to the sea below.

Buka was gone from her sight, now there was no island in the blue sea below. She wondered why her Bougainville was called 'one country' with the Papua New Guineans when there was no proof of closeness between them.

She remembered her flight from Taro airport to Honiara some years back. It was so beautiful how her Bougainville was connected to Choiseul, Santa Isabel and Guadalcanal. But now she was lost. The Papua New Guineans had indoctrinated Bougainvilleans with all the lies they had adopted and created for their own country.

The plane merged into some turbulence that surprised her. Below she could not see any further because of the thick clouds. So she mumbled a prayer to God for her safety on the plane and in the land of the strangers ahead.

Warm tears rolled down her cheeks as she envisaged her mother sitting and crying at the Buka runway.

"Dear God," she prayed in tears. "Protect and guide me for I am the mother of Bougainville; a Bougainville woman who is still in pain and in need of freedom. Let me be the light of the future for my people who perished in the war against exploitation and those who are still forced to dance to this exploitation and indoctrination. Amen."

Erereng – *'redskin' in the Nasioi language.*
Si damaiko simenang - *Oh, you are leaving me, my love.*
Tampa sikuru darabaing - *commit yourself to your studies.*

3
DANCING IN A REDSKIN'S ARAWA

Amiau listened attentively to the sound of dried leaves and twigs littering the forest floor being crushed. Is this another silly wild dog wandering about she wondered?

"Bekenenu, is it you there?" she called out to her husband who she had just left further uphill inspecting their cocoa plot.

No answer came so she ignored the strange sound that was now gone and lowered her body into the hole she had dug tracking the huge yam tuber.

Now, a heavy foot was approaching her, crushing the dried leaves of the galip-nut and cocoa trees that hosted her yam. She ignored it.

Exhausted, with strained back, she dragged her head carefully out and spotted through her armpit not a black foot but, a heavy red-skinned foot of a New Guinean about to attack her. A rapist!

"Oiiiii, Bekenenu! Bekene…nu, ere'rengkong mosika," she screamed hysterically for survival.

They rolled holding onto each other downhill under the consoling shade of the cocoa trees. Amiau's muscular body was determined to liberate itself from her New Guinean rapist who was struggling to strip her.

As they hit a rotting bole she removed the infiltrator's sweat ridden palms and screamed: 'Help! Someone help!'

"Where are you?" Bekenenu called.

"Here!"

To Amiau's relief, the redskin darted off as the sound of running feet crushing the dried out cocoa leaves littering the ground drew nearer. Bekenenu swiftly approached the scene angry and ready to attack.

"Did the infiltrator bastard redskin touch you?"

"No,'"Amiau sobbed in shock.

Bekenenu tracked the foreigner with his bush knife down Kirokai Creek but withdrew early in fear of being killed by the redskin strangers in the land.

"Did you see or talk sense to the redskins?" old Taruko asked, with sympathy as Bekenenu returned with sweat freely rolling off his balding head.

"Ee, send me not into the red ants' camp for I shall return to Dokotoro as a firefly, uncle," Bekenenu sniffed brusquely as he sat on a mat of dried leaves.

Taruko eyed the couple thoughtfully. With the sun burning above their heads, their anger and self- pity was like magnesium burning in the night sky.

The redskins' town below was booming with heavy traffic. Taruko's aged eyes were locked on the great Arawa General Hospital. Slowly, his blinking eyes left the hospital and crept up Siopa Place and then settled at his feet.

"This was our land when I was a child," he said, wiping away tears, "but today it is the redskins' land, not ours." The couple listened like children adsorbing every bit of parental advice.

The grey haired prudent one sneezed and continued, "When their government muddled us and impertinently began the Panguna mine, planes and ships brought them day by day into our land. Here they make the money to build their country that is so far away across the sea."

"Really true," Amiau spoke after a long silence, "all the schools in this town belong not to us, all is for these foreign rapists, looters and destroyers of Bougainvillean harmony. At Toniva, Kieta, down here, at Loloho and Panguna, it is they who roam with absolute freedom and we are the dogs with our tails glued to our bellies."

"That's why I often say, don't be a lone bird in the tree for a sick dog to harm you. This race of people is parlous to our Solomon ways," Taruko said, and skinned an areca nut to ease his mind.

"When you were children I saw that fading sun before you. As this town was developing the white man feared not the Bougainvilean but rather was afraid of the redskin that raved in the night like bats."

The trio climbed - a troop of defeated warriors - up the Sirovii brae for the ridge infested with swaying orange trees. Like those fruit trees, fear snarled and scurried in the air that they breathed into their lungs. Bougainville was not theirs.

Taruko spat red betel nut phlegm into the bush with a sigh and calmly called out to the couple, "As long as the New Guinean is on our land, there will be fear and tears."

Mosika - red skinned dog.

4
THE TONGARE LOVE

You know barau, down the length and breadth of my home valley, Tumpusiong; I was a popular wild and sexy dancer of the Friday night parties. Drinking was my trade.

People right across Kieta also referred to me as a sex maniac since I did earned myself some degree of fame with women here and there, from Panguna to Arawa and up the Bovong river valley; they knew me.

My reputation was getting worse every day; wherever I went, people would greet me as: "Good morning, bottle," or otherwise: "Good afternoon, doro'bauko." Pornography was also one issue I was known as the master of, as distributor and promoter. Whether all this was right or wrong, that was my name that the wind blew around everywhere.

Regretful, you know. As sanity slowly bloomed in me I began developing a tendency to reject, right from the core of my loins, such ugly tags. One can say that such cabbage is taciturn, but I think it isn't so - it's a calamity. A disaster I crowned myself with because of my irresponsible ravings originating from the dark side of my conscience.

Besides, I had dreams - whether it will gain fruition or not, I had them - to become the first president of the future nation, the Republic of Bougainville.

Such good ambitions had being consistently forcing me to dig down deep; lose some sleep, just to get to know more about myself as a person. Should I still remain the beacon of such dirty notions? The answer was "No".

To rid myself of all these odious prejudices, I slowly began looking for a girl - a full blooded Tumpusiong girl in the few clans available: the Bompo, Barapang, and the Bakerang. Within my clan, the Basikaang, I was not allowed to forage for sex; exogamy, denied what we in *Tok Pisin* refer to as '*wantok kaikai wantok*'.

My search, you know, was met by the most inferior clan across the valley of Tumpusiong, the Bompo. There I found one girl - perfectly shaped by her creative papa, nurtured well by the doctrines founded by Helen White and workaholic because of the harsh dictates of the great Kavarong river - our river. It all happened this way.

It was a day in August, 2006, the year of plenty as I now know it; that I, with my head packed with dirty mental graphics, was leisurely strolling about in the Tabarunau Trade Store grounds with a stupid friend who never hides his emotions. We knew the fact that there were girls that pass through this avenue, every afternoon out of the gold fields. So we waited, at least to win one or just to comment on her ways or to attract her out into the bush.

In the course of our aimless sauntering, we gave way to a passer-by making her way out of the trade store.

"E, Muruona, where are you off to?" my escort, Kontemoi asked her; closely eyeing her every bodily motion.

"*Osi dei'o*. Good day to you." She passed us with openness so sweet and a guilty smile.

"*Kongto bakaang*, era," Kontemoi murmured, his eyes fixed on her free-moving buttocks that seemed to deny the presence of the plain laplap with which she was covered.

She was lost down the camber to the Tongare pipeline that long ago transported the mining waste from the dead Panguna mine. She was heading to the hamlet of Damabori. A hamlet that was attractive to the local populace of boys since it housed some of the best looking girls in Tumpusiong.

For us, the proverb: 'out of sight; out of mind' was not workable as we stood there watching her, manoeuvre her way slowly through the open gravel and rock land. For me, I was thinking about her too much: what could she have said if I had asked for the thing? How would she have responded if I was making love to her? But these were just illusions, for she was not there. So, we got ourselves seated for gossiping.

To our surprise, however, she reappeared just like an apparition and headed straight back to the store.

"E, beauty, back again?" Kontemoi quipped with interest.

"I left something over there, in the store. And what are you two still doing here?"

"Waiting for you baby girl.."

She was just startled by that, and cursed Kontemoi with a laugh and headed straight for the store.

So, there was not a hint of problems with her. We could try out asking if she could love me till it hurts. My heart beat doubled as I saw her preparing to depart. But I was fixed on not losing this chance.

"Kontemoi, I am going to asked her for a minute in the bush, era," I told my friend. We moved down to the Tongare drop at a snail's pace.

"Do just that. She's cute, you know. Let's wait for her here...*Anikapeto*, era." Kontemoi began laughing restlessly.

Muruona moved slowly towards us. My heart got hot and felt like jumping out of my chest; and you know what, my lips were trembling as well. Did she note this? Who knows, but I decided not to let go this chance blossoming right here.

"Era, Muruona." I called her and took a deep breath to steady myself as she responded by halting in front of us. "Is there any space?"

Her lips produced no answers. I just stared at her in disbelief as the world was spinning right there, between us in fury. What was wrong? Whatever it was I'd at least caught myself before things got worse or out of hand.

There no words to keep the confrontation going, she was badly disturbed so we all went off in our separate ways. So, I was not attractive to her, was I?

A few days later, I was resting – or rather daydreaming - in my domicile when one of my *mamas,* who was also a student, began smiling at me from a good distance after arriving from school.

"Era Sisione, what did you do to Muruona?" she asked me, laughing and pouting.

I was infuriated. My insane idiocy had opened me to the public ears, again. I was getting mad at myself and condemned her.

"What did she say?" I glanced hard at my mama.

"She said you asked for space," young mama was giggling, "and that has hurt her as she considers you as her brother."

"Oh I did that for fun, era," I lied. Mama just laughed and walked towards the kitchen hut.

I was frustrated a little - not that badly, though - because such experiences were part of my everyday life.

It was raining that Sunday morning. From Kavarongnau, my hamlet, the Kavarong River showed signs of easing flood. On the opposite bank, around Dutumami, a few people though were panning for gold; as were, a few cockatoos that were noisily searching for ripe fruit.

The church bell rang as I entered the partially crowded classroom church. Kontemoi, who was already seated, informatively smiled as I approached his desk-pew.

"Era Muruona was very sad about that incident, you know," Kontemoi began as the sing-along was gaining momentum. "Last Friday I met her with Lisa and they scolded me. The other thing is that that *bisi noru'ku* Kasa is taking things seriously."

You know my mind was not connected with something divine, right there; it was there, amidst those beautiful - to the village standards - girls of the Bompo at Damabori.

Strange, but an interesting development had come my way through this stubborn Muruona. I was thinking, Kasa

- the daughter of this popular Tumpusiong's chainsaw man - wants it from me. In actual fact, you should know that around this time of my life I was deciding to say no to promiscuity.

To me, she was worth snoring by her side under a thick blanket. I had seen her before. Once while on a drinking spree at Pirurari, on a Saturday, I stared at her. She had a perfect body, especially those extra-large buttocks - wide hips - compared to her whole body. I liked it, very romantic.

And Kontemoi summed it all, after listening to all the preaching of the church elder, he whispered: 'And you know what, this Kasa said that Muruona was not fit for you and she is better suited to you.'

I was dumbfounded in the middle of the prayer session. Was Kasa a blessing and a potential partner for life? I thought so since that day.

In the distant Sipuko, a rooster gave its morning cry at early dawn on one of those rare days of early August when the night sky was overthrown by twinkling stars and meteorites.

With a few bats infiltrating the harmony sown by the growing twilight, there I was, sitting on the lawn thinking about that b*ompo'rikonang*, Kasa. How am I going to contact her and avoid discovery by my other girlfriends? Letters were the only way out. But not directly, I needed another medium.

And that medium, I knew, was my young student *mama*. Kasa was her classmate and best friend.

So at that dawn I began writing before my *mama* woke up to walk the lengthy distance to Darenai Primary School. I just used an exercise book page to write my words in the simplest English. I wrote telling Kasa I was romantically inclined for her. That was all. And my *mama* carried the message for me.

And for a full week, I waited in anticipation of a good

feedback, you know. Dirty thoughts - situations, in local *Tok Pisin*, we refer to as, *'tingting pussy'* - ruled my mind. I was thinking of Kasa, badly. I also lost interest in my other girls. Kasa was all I wanted, no matter what.

Every time I thought about her, I listened and sung alongside my stereo the song by the Backstreet Boys, *As Long as You Love Me*. Especially, the chorus, it got me the most. So, I sang the words much louder: *I don't care who you are, Where you from; don't care, What you did, as long as You love me.*

So, what I wanted came the way I wanted. My mama slipped a note into my hands one afternoon and it read:

> *Darenai Primary School*
> *C/- Bougainville*
> *11 August 2006*

Dear Sisione,

Good morning or good afternoon, taim yu kisim dispel leta. Mi laik tokim yu olsem bai mitupela pren. Tasol, yu noken niusim olsem mitupla ipren, nogat mama blong yu korosim mi.

Noken tingting planty tumas na slip gut tasol bikos drem blong yu ikamap tru.

Tenk yu
Kasa.

This is the one for life, I thought. That night, with the folded piece of paper resting on my bare chest I went to sleep. The night was the best in my life as were the dreams it provided of Kavarongnau hamlet.

The sun, though glowing, was setting over the Darenai ridge as I stood and gazed at its glaring reflection on the Damabori roofing iron. Many people pushed wheel barrows here and there on the rocky banks of the Kavarong racing against the approaching night with their alluvial gold panning stuff.

"E, Sisione what are you doing here? On a date?" Januaries interrupted my thoughts. He was returning from school. "I left Kasa and her friends down there at the volley-ball court. She is the right girl, barau."

For several days - after a few failed dates - I was wondering if Lisa had expressed herself honestly in those sweet words in her childish *Tok Pisin* letters. So, I was planning to squeeze the lemon out; and here was that opportunity.

"Why didn't you pat her buttocks?" I asked him. My brother was to glean how she would react now she had committed to me. "You must do that. Caress her anywhere at will."

"Damn, is this is an order?" the little Januaries smiled and radiated jubilation, "I'll start off tomorrow."

"Tell her that Sisione is taking on that mountain girl, Rachel, as you are not giving him the thing he wants," I added as we walked back home.

Januaries was very interested, though, underage and without *sitapu* he seemed to know everything about love and its making.

"Have you made love to her yet?" he asked.

"Yes,' I lied, "down there at the three cemented tyres outside her home."

He took hold of my left hand, "Just at her doorstep? You must be a ghost and cross this Kavarong in the nights when it is very cold and dangerous."

"Well, for a girl you can cross rivers, mountains and oceans, no matter what." We paced on for the Kavarongnau elementary school where Januaries was dwelling with my brother.

Two days later Januaries handed me a letter from my big girl, Kasa. She, you know complained about Rachel and my lies that I had made love to her. *Sapos yu pren wantaim, Rachel?* it read in one paragraph, *pren wantaim em tasol na maski long mi.*

"Dear sweet heart," Januaries read aloud the welcome

address. "So, her other name is Essam, *yu tok*. She signs off, *By Essam*. Why didn't she write, *By, Mrs. Sisione. Ol meri tu ya, save laik staiüm nabaut.*'

I neatly folded the exercise book page and fumbled it into my back pocket and we disbanded.

"I felt her buttocks and they are like a mattress," Januaries said to me, laughing one day. For him, I thought, fingering Kasa was an achievement for an underage bastard.

"Anyway brother, the world is changing every day under our very noses - sexism boom. The toddler out there will soon start making love before a parent realizes what is going on."

Though I was hurt, I acted as if enjoying his talk, as usually. "How did she - your wife - react?"

"She just walks on. Kontemoi had Botuto engaged, as well."

"This is a fucking animal; a dirty moll," I concluded and left Januaries for my new hamlet, Poarunau.

Ahead on the brae, above Poarunau, a garden fire was belching out thick clouds of smoke. "He will have something to eat, tomorrow," I thought to myself, as I, a prick, just wander around after girls' grubby pubes.

Later in the middle of the night, I began to write a letter denying all these allegations. I told her that I was just perfect.

The room was packed with young and old people with square eyes. With the film *Rush Hour* on, kids were mingling around telling each other the movie story ahead. Everyone listen attentively to the video owner's son whom I observed, had some sort of a power base to talk more.

Across Tumpusiong this was now the children's culture. The motion pictures told them stories. To them, even the relationships between the actors was readily known.

I was frustrated but remained silent. My eyes were on

the screen whilst my ears paid close attention to the various children's talk under the heat of the setting sun.

"E, Januaries, *kamap nau*?" someone asked from behind me.

"Em…. And did you see Sisione around here?" I over-will heard. "He is over there; anything important? Otherwise you put him into trouble." The man giggled to a halt because the movie was at an important part right at the moment.

Januaries just laughed and squeezed his way through the mass of people for me. Some children complained of this intrusion.

"E, what's up?" I whispered, "What did she say?"

"You fuckin shit," Januaries lowered his voice into a whisper. "Her friend, Lisa, wants you right now, by 7 'o'clock at the Tongare pipeline. She will be waiting."

I looked back at the crowd to see if anybody was interested at my sudden leaving but nobody seemed to be; captured as all were carried away by the stunt filled movie; not even Januaries, he was far away.

My ramble was more like a gait through heaven. The pain on my soles from the sharp edged gravel was not there as I sped up my pace in the dark. Fireflies, which in Kieta we believe are the spirits of the dead behaved strangely at my approach but I just swore at them and passed on.

Hamlet Tengona, on the opposite bank of the Kavarong River was alive. People were laughing inside their *kavoros*. Maybe, the delicious smell from their cooking pots was worth chuckling at whilst I was advancing through this night for our friend Lisa without any dinner menu. A moment with my love was my food for the long sleep.

As I passed the final corner of the road, lights at the Tabarunau store came into view, just a mere two hundred or so metres away. I checked my watch, it was half six, so I slowed my pace.

A lone bat loosened its grip from a tree above me and surprised me. "You evil bastard," I condemned it loudly and watched it heading for the Bori hamlet on the opposite bank. Maybe, his girl was there, somewhere.

My eyes scanned the area of barren land created for us by Bougainville Copper Limited many years ago. All was lifeless gravel, rocks and silt from the Panguna Mine and a few fireflies snooping about from the cemeteries. There were not supposed-to-be intruders in my secret love life. My wrist watch alarm rang. It was 7 'o'clock, my moment to tour heaven with Kasa. We could make love there as angels stared in pure wonder.

Unsuccessfully, I was forcing my poor eyes not to blink and in due course my toes were crushed on a lone piece of rock. I swore, but then laughed when a funny thought came into my mind: if Kasa's father knew of our date, we could be in hell. He could be chasing us all over this mining-made desert with his chain-saw screaming an inch from our rumps.

Standing over the edge of the Tongare gravel washout was the mining waste pipeline that acts as a bridge over the Tongare tributary; it was now clear just like the heavens above. Thank God, I told myself. And where are you Kasa?

I stood still for a moment leaving every task at hand to my pair of eyes. My sight searched with every joule of energy the Tabarunau side of the Tongare creek. No-one, I was thinking without knowing Kasa was already in a lone cluster of elephant grass trying to recognize me from my wandering movements.

Recognizing me in the murky darkness, she and her friend Lisa stood up. Surprised, unprepared for this, I in turn made a quick turn-around and slowly paced back.

If this is Kasa, I began my prayer with my heart beating wildly, she must follow.

It ended up the way I wanted it. She and her companion darted to my side as my whole being perspired with joy upon recognizing who these girls were.

I stared into the heaven: "Thank you." The stars were twinkling in response. They knew it; the Poarunau lone boy is now with his girl so don't bother him.

No one spoke as both of our hearts were beating twice the normal rate. Every corner of our brains had love scenes. We needed to kiss and make it true.

Though, I knew Kasa had received my letter I asked hopelessly just to start up our conversation, "Era, did Januaries give you my letter?"

"Yes," she chuckled to my relief.

My mind searched for many stories but none available upon sensing her closeness. I unconsciously placed my right hand over her shoulders and directed her to sit on a bare rock.

Seeing our quick union, Lisa began to distance herself.

"Era, Tobonu, come get my bilum and umbrella," Kasa called her friend. She responded swiftly, and out into the dark she was lost, again.

"Era, there's no rain but your umbrella is here," I laughed, now my body glued to hers.

"I haven't made it to the village just because I was waiting for the lone boy from upstream Kavarong to come."

"I am just —," I was interrupted.

"Promise me, you will marry me," she begged like a child, asking his father for chocolates.

"Kasa, I started befriending you for that word 'marry'," I said holding her tightly. "But, your parents are mad over our relationship."

Kasa kept silent searching for words and said, "They'll die trying to stop us."

My heart leapt and my moist lips smashed into hers in a desperate kiss. The gravel we were on came to life as we lost our sitting position and began to roll over each other.

In the silent darkness we were making love by the purling Kukutai brook off the brawling Tongare creek. Our bodies engaged in perpetual hooting of pleasure without Damabor knowing it. Thank you, gods.

Kasa was unconscious and laid flat on the silt. She knew she was no longer a girl. I sat beside her and waited as she regained strength.

"Kasa, remember you are mine, no matter what," I whispered into her ears. We hugged and began kissing.

"I am dreaming we'll be making love all over the banks of Kavarong," I whispered. 'We'll go as far as Ipukeitave and Darenai school lawns, too, darling."

"Dako otong" she chuckled.

Our lips met once again in goodbye. This was a night, I told myself, never to erase from my mind.

Mama — *mother; in the Nasioi kinship system a person's aunt is also referred to as 'mother'.*
Doro'bauko - sex maniac.
Wantok kaikai wantok — incest.
Osi dei'o - towards home.
Kongto bakaang - sexually suitable.
Anikapeto - there she comes.
Bisi noru'ku - big buttocks.
Bompo'rikonang - girl of the Bompo clan.
Tingting pussy - sex thoughts.
Sitapu - pubic hair.
Sapos yu pren wantaim Rachel, pren wantaim em tasol na maski long mi - If you are with Rachel, then let it be her.
Ol meri tu ya, save laik staiäm nabaut - Oh girls and their styles!
Kamap nau - just arriving?
Kavoros - kitchen huts.
Dako otong - it's up to you.

5

TEARS FOR MY BOUGAINVILLE

A fine eddy of cloud crowned the gigantic boulder, Ovoring; yonder east of my Topinang village. Ovoring's base was the source of the brawling Dangkua River that provided a water supply throughout the year - across all seasons; and in, good times and bad times.

We have sacrificed our lives to defend this beautiful land of clouds and pure greenish mountains; and the jet-black people - the owners of this land.

I, like many others, those that survived to live on, and those that perished with time, sacrificed for the cause, fought the bitter war for the liberation of the Bougainville people, the environment and the culture from foreign relegation. We took up arms, those lethal weapons, to wage the bloodiest crisis of the Pacific after World War Two to save our land from marauders, the Papua New Guineans and Conzinc Riotinto.

From coast to coast, we brawled with the infidels. On that detrimental Bougainville Strait, that foe infested expanse of Solomon Sea, men bled to their fate. Upon those untamed jungles and ridges we struggled on and on; day and night.

Yes, Bougainville, had to be free from all forms of false political indoctrination; and all other styles of oppression that are heard of under our gracious sun.

But these days, I sometimes sit and wonder, in a stream of tears how things have gone since. The way it shouldn't: why all this irresponsibility? Where did we go wrong? Were we freedom fighters, or just a bunch of liars under the scourging tropic sun?

We claim to have buried the hatchet, but that old staccato rattle of the gun is still out there; scarring those innocent people who long to feel peace and witness progress on their trouble-torn island.

Brothers my heart is in my mouth as I watch our leaders under intense stress - like knocking off work to carry bricks; that is nothing but a result of our irresponsibility and stupidity.

The sun was just overhead and the distant mountains were shimmering as Damparu exhausted himself weeding his kaukau plot. Regularly he was slashing grass with a knife and piling the unwanted plants. Uprooting and piling, he went, paying no heed to anything; but deep in thought, he was.

Streams of sweat trickled down his solidly built body. The sweat was endless. Often droplets were mistaken for a fly on his thick lips and cautiously, he would fold his lower lip to scare off the intruder. But upon realizing his mistaken effort, he swore loudly, often surprising his wife at the far end who was also busy mounding.

"What's all this bestial swearing for?" his wife asked once, out of boredom.

His balding face glittering with sweat, Damparu, told himself to hop the topic. Let the sweat thing sleep. The recent stealing of the UNDP car in town by armed thugs was making him sick; so, it needed to be voiced to his dear woman.

He knew she wanted some talk; some serious blathering to sweep aside the exhaustion of the garden work. Would she ever be willing to shoulder the political pain he was wondering. She loves, after all, talking politics like a man of Bougainville does.

He momentarily halted his unearthing and piling and looked, pleadingly at his wife, Toboinu, who was now seated under a shade of a banana tree. He stretched with a yawn as if he was just waking from sleep.

"This shit...foolish nephew of mine, Ori, is making me sick with shame," he said, bending to his unearthing; heaving and piling work, again. "He partook in the UNDP stealing in town. Someone, I forgot who, told me yesterday." He impatiently grasped his knife and slashed hesitantly, and added, "Not that he intended, he told me that when I asked him. The Kongara men, his former fighting friends, asked him to help them out because they don't know how to drive; *kongto, kanukanu nangka!*"

Toboinu stood and slashed her *dimmiri* at the worn out leaf of the banana. "Why did he help them, that insane Ori?"

"Because they hired him with cartons of beer to get the vehicle out of town where they can learn to drive, I think."

"Oh, down with those scoundrels and.....but this Ori was so insane to assist those bastards; sentimentally foolish." She bent to pick up dried out banana leaves, as she continued, "He has cocoa he can sell to help him satisfy his appetite for beer. Why appease those people's self-centred hunger for crime?"

"Birds of a feather flock together," Damparu babbled valiantly. "This incident makes Ori a double skinned boy. His laziness is only suppressed by our presence seems to me. We'll get their old commander, Dunsimora, to sort them out before the lacerating guilt of their deeds pricks our throats further."

"Do just that." She snapped.

In his preoccupation, Damparu sat in his recess of slashed grass idly watching a gang of crows lazily cackling. They were obviously sun bathing at the fringe of his garden. To his displeasure, their singing turned hysterical, and in a slide of seconds they dispersed in fear. Every noise was submerged by the cackle of their fright.

From behind, Toboinu knew someone was intruding into their territory. "Is someone coming that way, and disturbing the birds?"

"Hopefully so." He nodded his head. "Maybe Dunsimora and his family are bound to the garden."

It was I, Dunsimora, the very same person coming that way. As I approached him I saw relief in his arched broad face. From his squatting position under the calm of the undergrowth he twinkled with hope in a sea of hopelessness.

"*Baramang*, it's good that you came," he blurted out eagerly.

He was like a desperate child in need of attention. Comforting and some prayer petitioning, he needed.

"What's bothering you, *barata*?" I asked, gibbering and bending instantly to free one of my toes from the stinging black ant - a *pika*.

His wife called to us. "*Anangka*, pawpaw *aung*, have it and then you can swim in your sea of politics," she said with a laugh.

I chuckled back loudly: "*Enang ani, teu kapeto*. Good for health." Damparu just sat idly. Such extremity I'd never seen in him before. He was like an invalid finding solace in me.

"*Aung ee*, did you hear the gun fire in town last....last...ha," Damparu exhaled for a rightful time..... Wednesday night?"

I was interested. "Yes. What was it then?"

"Our nephew Ori and a number of Kongara fellows stole the UNDP car; that white Hilux. It's now somewhere in Doreinang." His hairy right hand snatched a kaukau leaf. With its stalk attached, he had it near his fat nose; examining it hesitantly.

A spasm of regret ran down my spine. At the same time, I was feeling guilty and exposed. Was I involved? Why not! I was Ori's commander before.

My gaze was on his leaf. "Oh, my men, why are they so lawless these days? They act as if they have no land to sow and reap the stainless fruit of their labour."

Studying his leaf, he just nodded his thick lip. Once or twice, came a shrug as I talked on. "Obvious liars we were. Poor Bougainvilleans! Calling ourselves freedom fighters, but we are irrational betrayers of freedom. What do you think? *Kanu kanu nangka kongto*!"

"We should start killing those rascals, those *dangkong* freedom men, one by one." He gave a hopeless laugh.

"You'll worsen the situation; that's an opprobrious act which will ensnare the peace process." I chuckled lazily.

"Oh, hornbills!"

Both of us looked into the sky. A pair of hornbills were heading east, towards Dokotoro village. Yonder, the sea was pure bluish. Only few island points made a contrast. But, in its own way, still it was nice and immaculate. Fine. A salubrious day.

"Dunsimora, *eeng*," Damparu cut in solemnly, "*Onou ama bore sipa mo maung ee.*" He slitted the leaf in half; dropped the right part and began fingering the sticky sap as he rattled on, "In the beginning there was a clean fight. The whole of Bougainville rallied behind us. Then came the 1990 ceasefire, there we messed everything up. Opportunities lost! Bougainville was divided. We turned on each other. *Piaru nuka.*"

A lone mosquito bit him; he paused and gave it an open palm slap. Dead; he cursed it and continued, "After years of striving, we created this peace process. Fragile as it is, we still ignore everything and pursue our insignificant follies. Leaders sacrifice for our good, but we create for them more complications. Who knows when those few sane and wisdom-filled leaders will die, what then shall these good-for-nothings do? Bastards! Don't you think, we will attain independence not at all." He spat in front of his toes and stared at it in wonder. Maybe he was trying to figure out how many millions of microbes were there in that soupy spittle.

"*Bera Ori, are ontong?*" I asked, swallowing the last gobbet of my juicy pawpaw.

"I berated him so he fled to his papa's place, Karikira. He's there." His head dropped further, watching an army of ants working out a new trail.

"We need to return that vehicle back. I just can't handle the pain of public gossip or become a community spittoon. This is Topinang's first lawless involvement and must be sorted out. Am I not a signatory to the Peace Agreement?'

"We'll do that hand in hand." Damparu got to his feet. His wife, laden with a knapsack, was heading home.

"Yes, I won't permit myself to a lie or otherwise I find it much easier to do it at a second time." I lazily misquoted the words of Thomas Jefferson.

The sun was low above Pavaire village in the distance. A pleasant stream of insect stridulating, the chirping of crickets and the regular rasping of cicadas wrapped us up. Birds were settling for the night that was approaching.

I abandoned what I wanted to do in my garden, my visit would not be worthwhile since Damparu's wrist watch was reading half five. Beside the hills I still had to ascend were too forbidding and it would be night too soon. I decided to accompany the couple homeward.

"Bereai nanu narung, osiape."

Sleep was no way near that night. Foreign was peace. The shrilling of the insects outside was no longer that soothing lullaby that I was accustomed to.

But in the adjoining room my wife, Amio and our two children snored calmly. They were peacefully at ease. An owl hooted a dedication of songs to them. I listened restlessly as it paid homage to my unborn child and pacified his mama but not me and my political headaches.

"My child, this is not the kind of Bougainville you are supposed to be born into," I said into the night. "No freedom here. Men abuse authority here. Guns speak their words. Maybe when I am gone, then, your kind of Bougainville shall dawn. But still nobody knows when and how."

I sat up, restless and perspiring. To an endless flood of thought I meditated. I was a monk in the night, lonely in prayer. How are we to tame these irresponsible youngsters? We fought to defend this land, but now they see nothing good in it. They cry for free handouts. Miracles! Oh, gods, no labouring under cocoa trees, as I do.

In the dimly lit room my gaze fell on my two weapons, two M16 assault rifles which I had kept back after sending the rest away in containers at the dictate of the Peace Agreement. They were absolutely idle. Harmless they seemed; but they painted me as a fighter - the fearless killer beyond the fringes of Topinang.

I had purposefully kept them, this sanguinary merchandise, though, as a BRA commander, I felt guilty of playing pranks with the Peace Agreement. But, to me, the guns had an intrinsic value. One belonged to my brother, Bade, killed in an engagement with our enemy, the Papua New Guineans. As a memory, it was worth keeping. The other, was my first won rifle. I had shot a damn redskin soldier in Panguna to get it; henceforth, it had made me well known and respected across Bougainville.

But my reputation, spotless as it was, now losing control of my men? Not all were that troublesome. It's this lone bird, my own blood, Ori that has defamed me. My men were responsible cocoa farmers on the land - the land they defended. They are labourers, making money for the government - our government.

A cool breeze filtered through the window; roughly swishing the curtain. Imagination forcefully dragged me back to those killing moments, way back in 1992 outside Arawa. Here, my brother, Bade's blood was sacrificed for the thousands of Bougainvilleans, the good and the bad.

That day, those fatal hours, myself, backed by my beloved brother and others, ambushed and mopped up a truck load of red-skinned soldiers. Our arsenal of weapons was added to but the price was the tragic loss of a loved one.

Warm tears trickled down my cheeks in the dark. Bade was a man of freedom, whenever he discovered any mischief among our fighters, he effaced that dirt-on-the-trail.

"What are we fighting for," he would attack verbally, looking the perpetrator straight in the eyes, "our prestige and power? Greed? Sex and Luxury?"

"Think about our Bougainville Revolutionary Army.

The word 'Revolutionary', why did we place it in the centre rather than leaving it as Bougainville Army or something else? Always abide your actions to that term. Consistently, I mean. Otherwise, we are liars; first to our people, then to the rest of the world who are watching us."

These were his words whenever he confronted any form of ignorance and irresponsibility among our fighters.

I sobbed bitterly for my daring brother. We were real brothers-at-arms during those days. We fought together, cried together and rejoiced together.

At the first cock cried, just outside my window, I laid down to rest; the remaining hours.

The sun was high when I woke up. Outside doves cooed over breakfasts of galip nuts.

I wouldn't have woken but the noisy prattling of my son interrupted me in my dream. I was seeing myself somewhere in a remote beautiful place; somewhere I was daringly longing to be.

"*Papa dararabai.*" he was artlessly jabbering, pulling at the seams of my bed sheet. "Papa wake up."

"Oh darling, you're disturbing me." I held his tiny left hand as we marched outside. The sun was refreshing.

The look on my wife's face was beseeching. I was bemused, of course, she saw that.

I lifted my boy and seated him calmly next to me inside the smoky cook house. "I am off to Doreinang today," I said.

"Oh, you'll get into hot water,' Amio said soberly, "don't you attempt that. Those people become awkward when they know they're wrong."

"We've got balls too, if they can remonstrate, then we can do that also." I chuckled with a tone of seriousness.

As we talked Damparu arrived and sat out on the porch. He heard our conversation. "We burn them up if they resist. I sent for Ori, as well, he'll be waiting for us at the town market."

She handed us our plates of food. "Go, but be

cautious, men. Let their comrade Ori do most of the talking. It's good that you sent for him." Amio disappeared in to the *kavoro*, then reappeared and added, "They are humans; anyway, just approach them properly. Damparu, you must use your best negotiating skills."

Carried away with the tasty rice and stew, he just laughed, "I'll just do that, woman. You'll see, we'll have the car back."

"Off then," Damparu said rinsing his hands. We ambled towards the car, calmly resting at the u-turn in the heart of our village.

I remained silent most of the time watching cousin Damparu's feet and hands artfully handling the pedals below; the gears, and the wheel. A child I seemed to the driver.

Ori, upon seeing us from the crowded market fought his way out and joined us. My spirit was lifted as we left the town.

Damparu accelerated despite the loud chugging the engine gave.

Am I a pendulum, blown here and there by the wind of circumstances I was wondering. As we passed the last corner into Aropa I shrugged off the thought and committed my spirit to the task ahead.

"Is everything going to be alright?" I was confident but wondered, are these souls really with me?

Damparu swept a glance at me, "Yes." Ori, just behind me, in the double cab; uttered not a word. But, his swift response to Damparu's call meant more than this silence.

Our old chugging vehicle made its way; nice and slow but comfortably. The gravel road had just recently been up-graded. Recent rain denied us from dragging behind a trail of spiralling dust.

I, as maybe were my partners, since a trip to this corner of Kieta was rare, were amazed. Hectares and hectares of cocoa and coconut palms stood with promises. Regularly, we spotted vanilla crops. Their minders just ignored us.

Then where do these law breakers come from? I was fumbling in thought. I know that anywhere the truth is that there is always dirt in every community flustering the harmony there.

I laughed hopelessly.

"What is it?" Ori, was quick out of his shell.

"Just that a small group of people will always blur the reputation of our communities." My right hand lifted and pivoted to hand him a newspaper. "Many people are here, in the cocoa plots."

"*Masika e aung.*" The two chorused and Ori guiltily added, "I am one of them; demons lie to us, so we go marauding."

Joy rollicked in my heart to hear Ori admitting his guilt. He was a sane man.

"Mistakes are always there to guide. Ipso Facto, we need to always admit our wrong doing and never repeat our folly." I said. Rapidly, I blinked back my tears. "The era of guns has gone now; we are in an era to war with Papua New Guinea at the meeting table."

I knew I was helping my young man and not leaving him in a lurch. But these people here? The first house came into view.

"Ori, where does Dutana dwell?" I asked.

For some reason my heart was behaving strangely. My pulse was a bit faster. I was struggling to keep back some degree of sangfroid.

"Here, is it?" Damparu looked back, as the engine died abruptly.

With a slight clang of the door, Ori was outside. He stood amongst locals a commanding witness. His stalwart built was imposing, I thought. But running a side glance our driver seemed staid, behind the wheel. Was fear settling in? Not so, he climbed out denying my analysis.

They chatted about the car as I stood, my right elbow resting on the warm bonnet, admiring the place.

Perfectly clean was the village. Crotons lined the

roadside and grew around the houses. The lawns were neatly mowed. Fruit trees were in abundance. What a fine place I thought.

Further right was the church. It was the largest structure in the village. So, Christianity was at the heart of this community and, what about Dutaona? A son of a respected pastor, but a culprit who I was seeking for the good of Bougainville, was what? Maybe father hadn't done enough?

Imperiously I march towards the church yard where a couple of children were frantic over the game of marbles.

"Where is Dutaona, then?" I asked an old man in front of me.

His wrinkled rotund face reddened. "They sent for him. He is said to be knolling kaukau on the other side of the Siianng River, commander."

The old man's look of fear never left me. Am I lacking finesse, I wondered, fixating beyond the church where they said Dutaona would come from.

Colly-wobbles caught me. Ori was not to be seen. Damparu was saturnine and leaning on his car bumper. Both of us were now breathing what felt like an unsociable air.

I looked Damparu straight in the eyes. "Where are they saying the vehicle is?"

"Just beyond the church."

"Let's go and …"

Dutaona appeared and fired a shot into the air and shouted with burning ire. "Nobody is taking this car back." The rifle, an M16, firmly fixed in his hands; ready. For the fighting we did; you people are yet to compensate us."

Damparu was already in the car. No-one was near, all had moved to secure positions. My mind told me that the villain over there was playing a scare-off game.

"You Dunsimora, you too must go home,' he shouted with acerbity. "You got nothing to do with this car."

I was irritated by the scornful words. "Who said that, I

am not going back to Arawa without that car? Your papa did not buy it." Cautiously I began to pace towards the church.

He fired two rounds. One straying bullet tore down a frangipani branch above my head.

"Don't move, or I'll kill you." He said and fired again. This time the bullet went into the ground next to me.

I hesitantly moved forward watching his hands and the rifle.

He moved past the church towards me, this time, the barrel directed at me. Should I run?

"Fuck your grandmother! Shoot him! Let me, his nephew watch as you kill him. Shoot him!" Ori screamed with boiling fury.

From a corner of the church he appeared. He's right hand stretched out with a pistol firmly clenched in the palm.

"Shoot my uncle." He demanded. "Or you want me to shoot you?"

To my horror Ori fired. The M16 landed on the grass.

I hurried towards them as the onlookers gathered to see the bloody drama of the men's stupidity.

In two vehicles we passed Aropa. Seagulls hovered high above the crushing waves looking for food.

Ori nursed his victim in Damparu's car as I, alone in tears of pity, drove the UNDP vehicle.

"Should we be called freedom fighters, or liars?' I asked, looking at the white breasted birds above. Tears were freely trickling down my cheeks.

No one was there to answer me, so I just sobbed out: "My Bougainville; my motherland, where am I taking you?"

From Toborai, Fokpok and Tausina islands appeared to comfort me. They were green and beautiful, drifting on a calm blue sea.

Kongto, kanukanu nangka - foolish bunch.
Dimmiri - an old rusty knife.
Baramang, - my little brother.
Barata – brother.
Pika - stinging red ants.
Anangka – hey! (plural).
Pawpaw aun - here (handing something).
Enang ani, teu kapeto - Oh, woman bring it over.
Aung ee – hey!
Kanu kanu nangka kongto - very foolish people
False.
Dangkong - false.
Dunsimora, eeng! – Dunsimora, hey!
Onou ama bore sipa mo maung ee – thinking about it and my head is aching.
Piaru nuka – we are poor people.
Bera Ori, are ontong – and where is Ori?.
Papa dararabai – papa, wake up.
Bereai nanu narung, osiape – let's go.
Kavoro - a kitchen hut.
Masika e aung - I agree with you.

6
ANGEL KOKOPO

The fire was crackling with burning heat. In response, the blackened kettle steamed so roughly that it opened its lid. Toton carefully placed a tea-bag in the half-open teapot and whistled a tune as he admired the water turning thick brown. The smell of tea was promising.

After breakfast, he sat grooming himself and singing a local song from his home island of Nissan, back in Bougainville. Over, the refreshing sensation of potent betel-nut mixed with chalky lime and tart pepper fruits, he sang loudly; his old pet, a cat was disturbed in his sleep and carelessly leapt out the window hurting its left ear.

Toton looked out the window; the road he was to employ was clear of the much hated drunkards that molested him so much on his unlucky Friday nights.

Intent, he marched into the bedroom; stood firm in front of the mirror, admiring himself in numerous postures; randomly smiling away.

The breeze blowing from the sea had become perfectly calm. White breasted terns were overhead with their peculiar cries; sounds he knew well from the time before he was crawling. The wristwatch alarm rang; it was nine o'clock when he lazily closed the door behind him and rambled towards town.

Toton was a grade eight dropout and a domestic servant working for a European businessman. To any ignorant Papua New Guinean, he was a nothing but a cheap labourer subjected to the Whiteman's wishes. But this couldn't be so, because the skin Toton had was too deep and sly. He was a poor man with a sugary tongue.

Despite earning a fortnightly wages of one hundred kina, mismanagement had its toll on him. Distant eyes could easily glean that the island boy, Toton, was a natural squanderer. Wherever and whenever, women were around his vicinity he spent without care.

But he didn't curse this squandering stigma in him even when his mismanagement struck him hard. If he looked for obvious tearing claws in his wallet these were his drink mates. He condemned them as simple red skinned parasites but whenever his wallet was packed he ran after them like a crying child after its papa.

In one of those Chinese restaurants, Toton sat munching away at his food. Fried rice with fried chicken pieces, seasoned with garlic and curry, were on his plate.

He purposefully sat in the corner where he stared at the people without being noticed easily. His table had three empty chairs while all the others were occupied by hungry people eating greedily.

"Excuse, can we take these seats?" a girl's polite voice, surprised him. Her right leg dragged back a chair.

"Oh sit…..sit," he managed to say, over a mouthful of rice, to the girls in familiar Kokopo High School uniform.

Toton's gaze set on the more beautiful girl of the pair seated directly opposite him. From her luscious skin, the scent of perfume disseminated. Her make-up looked flawless but she had a vacillating look on her face. Nevertheless, she was still an angel.

"Oh, girls my name's Toton—" he briefly, paused for a thought. Then, added, "What grades are you in, by the way?"

"Grade eleven………both of us," Susan giggled.

"Enjoy your schooling?"

"Sometimes," both girls sang like a choir.

"Well girls, you must be committed to your education." He began his cunning tactics of cajolery. "I was a student like you once. I graduated with a BA in accounting from the University of Papua New Guinea and now I've got a private business back home in Bougainville."

Susan was hypnotized by the lie of the island boy. She

was thinking that her dream of marrying a well-to-do person, like this handsome Bougainvillean, might come to fruition; only if she could ask for it, but she hesitated; though lust was creeping up her spine.

"What sort of a ventures do you undertake?" she asked.

To this question, Toton was instantly on Nissan Island looking for some sensual feedback. Answers that could at least enchant Susan for the hour she might set foot on Dolengan wharf with him and his nonentity fantasies.

"Oh, yes......I run a boat service between my island and the mainland, Bougainville. I......I've also got a store, a guest house and three vehicles that service the islanders of Nissan."

"So, are you now on holidays?"

"Not so, girl, I am just returning from a business trip to Perth. You might have learned about it in one of your lessons. It is in Western Australia. Am I right?"

"Yes" Susan enthusiastically answered.

From that lucky Friday Toton was a happy man wih his once-in-a-blue-moon success in winning a gullible Tolai girl's heart. Their dates began to become regular. Often Susan requested a night in the hotel where her boy was holidaying, but Toton just couldn't entertain that and expose his below-poverty-line status too early. That could shatter his dreams of marrying his angel, Susan, for he had just discovered that she was a money face. Having her pregnant before she discovered his dire living conditions was his goal. Resigning from his work and taking Susan home was paramount in his plans.

One day as they lay embracing each other under the cover of some swaying shrubs and bananas, Toton said "I am leaving on Thursday for Nissan. I am taking you with me. In the Solomon Queen we will sail away."

"Thank you." She kissed him hard. "Why not in a jet plane, love?"

"Simplicity is my culture, Susan."

Thursday found the couple standing on the bow of the

rakish Solomon Queen. It was dark and chilly. But there, they were, embracing each other for warmth. A beam from a nearby lighthouse caught them, but it was growing weak every second, as the ship gained distance.

Susan watched the lighthouse fading; from a tiny dot, it went to an absolute nothingness. She was saddened but the presence of her well-to-do lover, Toton, ebbed that intruding pain off. Together, they marched into their third-class cabin, bolted the door and slept.

At 2 am Toton woke. He checked Susan; she was snoring in deep sleep. So he too decided to feign sleep as he fumbled deep in thought.

His lies, so ghoulish and fretful as it now seemed to him, to win this queen, was tearing at his flesh. A storm of guilt and shame was scurrying in his brain. How was he to elucidate to her, that in his love for her, he had lied to get her? Would she accept that? He flustered. Properties, soon to be seen, were not his nor his family's. He was a poor fellow since birth. Answers to his doubts were not that near.

Beside him, Susan slightly jerked in sleep. Rather than love, a spasm of pain ran up his spine generated by fear. "Why......oh why, can't you last forever, night"? He told himself. He imagined how weak he would grow in the coming days once this woman discovered the truth of his life and started attacking him. Women are said to be emotionally powerful and his girl was no exception—she'll wear him down.

Sometime later, thinking her partner was asleep, Susan wandered outside leaving the cabin door partly ajar. Outside, the alluring view of the islands stunned her; so she darted in, with curiosity. "Wake up Toton. We've arrived!" She dragged him out of the bed.

As the vessel cautiously made its way through the passage, Toton, saw that nothing much has changed. Coconut palms danced to the wind from Balil, down to Dolengan to Gerei and back to him along the sweeping expanse of white sandy beach as usual.

This land retained itself. Sirot and Barahun Islets were guarding the entrance to the lagoon. Inside, Han Islet in the heart of the lagoon was there welcoming him. Nissan was that same old bone of living.

"What's that islet, feigning as chief of the heart of this lagoon?" Susan was asking.

"Han." He managed with a faraway look.

"Toton, are you sick? You look so depressed."

"Nothing; I just need some sleep," he lied and walked back to the cabin. Guilt was obvious in his looks.

Susan knew - it was naturally instilled in her - that a person, like Toton, bringing himself a lover from further afield, should be boastfully talking about his home as they approached. But something was wrong! Toton was behaving strangely; not so interested in his home and people. "Mountebank! Mountebank!" a tiny voice was calling from deep in her mind.

Is he really? She wondered, a mountebank? Oh, get lost, evil. He kept me financially nourished all through our courting.

But her evil still sang. Okay, time will tell, she told herself standing beside tacit Toton on the bridge shaking hands with a few of his relatives.

The ship, now safely moored, was a house; a floating house. Her crew were busy preparing her for the next night's trip through that unimaginable undulating expanse of sea to Buka and beyond to such places as Kieta and Buin. Susan listened to the talk.

"Oh, Toton, you've got yourself a woman, you say." A wantok commended him in local vernacular.

"A Tolai girl," Toton chuckled.

Though, she enjoyed the strangeness of this language, Susan was annoyed at not being part of the talk that Toton and his friends were locked into. Once or twice she gave a pusillanimous look towards Toton when the term, Tolai, was articulated. This was not because she feared something, but simply to express her deep frustration at being kept in the dark.

"It's about time we got home," she said purposefully to cut the prolonged conversation. "Where is this Siar, men?"

"Right up there," Toton pointed in a north-westerly direction to where a bluish pillar of smoke was climbing into the morning air, "where the smoke is."

"It's your mama, Toton, burning something very early. Go show her your Susan," Otima, Toton's friend said, reassuringly.

Susan was worried about the distance. "My eyes tell me that, I can't walk this distance. So, go fetch a ….."

Toton knew that she was requesting a car ride. He had lied to her about owning three vehicles; and in Otima's presence, it was not worth spilling it over; that would hurt his pride too early. He wanted his lies to creep over his island, starting off from his birth place, Siar. Not Tangmerek or any other village.

"Okay, let's go….go…..go" he interrupted, lifting a packed rainbow bag to his left shoulder. "Okay, Otima see you around sometime."

"It's a nice walk new Siar girl," Otima said, respectfully waving his free hand to Susan.

"Thank you, Otima."

Without a word and in an air of swooping confusion they walked. A good number of people, obviously Dolengan bound, passed them, with ignorant chuckles, good mornings and dullish smiles.

This further infected Susan's restless mind. People were clearly paying no heed to her and Toton, except that student, Otima. Why?

Susan lazily glanced at her wrist watch under the shade of some coconut palms as they were approached the place that Toton said was Tangmerek. It was half past eleven, and Siar was not that near yet.

Tangmerek's cluster of buildings interested her. In the glaring heat of the sun and the balmy sea breeze, everything was still idyllic. "Can one of this be Toton's?" she wondered, when a rusting red Hilux caught her attention. She was resting perfectly under a blooming white frangipani, with children gawking through the flowers at her. "This must be the place?" she thought.

"Toton, when are we to reach your cars, or your store and that fine cosy guest house of yours?"

"Oh, woman right across there," Toton pointed west with his left hand. "Out there in Balil."

People's attention was caught by the stranger, Susan, pacing like a frightened child beside Toton, their kinsman.

"Toton, send for a vehicle. Where are the trio, you have?"

"I forgot to tell you," Toton said; "one is too busy, and two remain idle with mechanical problems. Sorry."

Susan quickly ran an impulsive gaze over Toton; from his hair down to his unpolished stockman boots. At least, he was perfectly handsome! But his skin seemed too deep, and needed squeezing out. "Businessman?"

After marching under the scorching sun past the church, discoloured by salt spray, and the buildings of Sigon Catholic Mission and the impenetrable mangrove bush at the foot of thickly forested Hiuon Hill, they arrived at Siar.

The place looked deserted at first. But there was life. A number of children were playing on the fine beach shooting at the airborne gulls with clumps of dead coral.

"Mama, Toton!," a naked boy paused to get a clear picture, and then darted into the village shouting, "Toton! Toton! Mama, Toton….and a girl, mama."

Toton stood deathly still, despite, the jubilation of his relatives. His eyes and thoughts firmly fixed on Susan. Would her learning of the truth set him free? Or just drag him into a prison of shame? Would she start nagging?

The high covenant house, he told her, was not there. The properties he had told her about were illusions. His home was no way near the standards he had been boasting about in that Chinese restaurant back in Kokopo.

To a low hut, without stilts, they were ushered with joyful singing. Toton's fat and short mama wept with elation, as did her escorts.

The hut was a single room. The people said it was Toton's. It was far worse than Toton's descriptions of his living standards. The aged roofing iron made her sick, as did the discoloured wooden walls. Peeping inside, there were rats' droppings, everywhere. The spring bed she would be resting looked likely to fall apart if they were ever to make love on it. Shocked, she swished at her shirt and sat on the bench offered to her.

"Oh, Mountebank!" she nearly screamed in fury. Then she ordered a passing child to look for Toton, who was running from house to house laughing with his people. That he was avoiding her was obvious.

As Toton approached she said, "So...so, you lied to me, eh?" She was hysterical. Her voice was hoarse. "You lied and have ruined my life. What do you say?" Warm tears ran down her cheeks.

Without a word, Toton sat on the wooden bench. His head dropped and he trembled. "What's next?" he asked.

"You tricked me! You, skint swine!" She roared to the shock of the villagers, who came running to witness the sudden outbreak of rumpus.

Swiftly she lifted up a piece of timber and landed it hard on Toton's naked nape. He cried in pain and began jostling his way away as Susan struggled to free herself from the dozen gripping hands trying to calm her down.

She managed to slip out of their grasp as Toton came back seeking conciliation. Seeing a knife in a nearby boy's hand, she grabbed it. Seeing this and the fierce look on Susan's face the whole mass of people fled to safety. She gave a chase after the dastard, Toton. People followed the warring couple at a safe distance.

That night, with Toton hiding in the bush, nowhere to be seen, she sat by the soothing sound of the calm sea, her eyes, misty with tears; evaluating her recent life. She was too gullible and stupid, that evil Toton took her for a ride.

"I was a fool," she scolded herself, looking at her dark shadow cast in the light of the crescent moon.

A lone bat flew towards the main passage of the lagoon. It was calling her to follow him, beyond the silhouetted shapes of Banahura and Sinot islets to where her homeland, Kokopo, was calling her.

7

AMEAI COUNTRY

Sikanai removed his underwear and hung it on the clothes hook attached to the wall; he slipped into the shower cubicle and turned on the tap.

Cold water poured over his plump body as he gazed admiringly at himself covered with fine droplets of water.

He envisaged making love in the bath and wanted to call his wife but he abruptly saved the thought because he must be in the office early for his appointments. "Water can be an aphrodisiac, sometimes," he told himself and laughed.

The morning sun was glaring fiercely, but he strode on past the Arawa Heath Centre. Sick people and visitors alike marched reluctantly in and out of the main gate.

On the main street, leading to the town centre - the market, the fast mushrooming shopping centre and the administration offices - only a few strolled deep in thought over their worries.

There were also a few cars speeding up and down the town roads; their cargoes - those few passengers - looking dull like first-time-in-towns. The air that Sikanai breathed was also empty; absolutely lifeless and somewhat intimidating.

Arriving at his destination - a residential house; renovated and extended into an office building, housing the Kieta District Administration, the public library and so on - he walked intently up the flight of steps and was lost at the main entrance as if sucked in by an invisible whirlpool.

Bureaucrat Sikanai sauntered through the dimly lit corridor, his brown eyes sweeping the wall of notices. Nothing interested him much. But his ears absorbed something whose boldness suddenly angered him. He controlled the urge to pummel the speakers to the floor.

Two clients with their backs to him were skimming through a pile of papers, indulging in some heavy gossip. "These officers sit in this fine room and grow themselves pot-bellies, *bani pininangka*," The other laughing over the first comment snapped, "Yes, barau, these crooks - ." He was - to his dismay - interrupted by the clang of Sikanai's keys as he turned the door knob to his office.

"*Eh, mata ne*, Sikanai," one of them greeted him. There was guilt and uncertainty in his tone, he expecting Sikanai's obvious reaction.

"*Tampara*. Same to you," was all Sikanai, with his humble heart could manage as the door closed behind him.

In preparation for meeting the gossiping pair outside he cleared the folders he had left the day before on the table. Then he opened a drawer and pulled out a neat pile of papers to work on and a writing pad to note matters of significance.

He quietly reopened the door. Bending, he placed an empty carton against the door to keep it ajar.

The pair smiled. "*Areke eanangka?* Come inside," Sikanai called lazily letting his gaze drift over their movements and dress before opening the conversation.

Sikanai was Deputy District Manager. In the absence of his seniors any decisions he was to make must be based on merit and within the content of the public policy management frame work he thought. He was there to serve Bougainville and not his kinsmen.

When the pair was seated the elder of the two began, "Yes we came with these papers," he said, carefully selecting his words, "for you to give us some ideas and further assistance," He laid the file mechanically on the table.

Sikanai dragged the papers towards him. "What's this for *anangka?*" he asked, patiently looking at the cover of the typed work.

"*Era*, it's a proposal for a planned reconciliation between the Mearura and Kokore villagers who fought during the crisis. They have been in regular conflict since then." The youngest began his discourse. "So the elder mediators have come up with that and are now in search of government assistance to effect reconciliation."

The lecturing man - with a few grey hairs to indicate his age - sounded very much like a professional negotiator. He seemed the type with enough profound ability to win any endeavour and impose drastic changes in his trouble-torn Bougainville.

"You know Sikanai; reconciliation is a must for us Bougainvilleans," he sighed, then, "if we are to advance further - ." The shuffling sound of feet outside distracted him.

He quickly collected his thoughts since bureaucratic Sikanai was still occupied, browsing with interest, "Yes we have signed a Peace Agreement but to me, it's an external covering. What's important is the small - as we might think - problems we have among ourselves; between families, between brothers, between clans and so on," he concluded abruptly seeing that Sikanai had completed his reading and was for some reason sighing.

Sikanai eyed them meditatively. He was a hunting eagle waiting for his prey. Then his gaze was diverted to a trapped bee in the window screen. It was struggling to get through the fly wire but its attempts were futile. The scene forced him to consider nipping the insect.

"Anyway, *anangka*, how many Kokores and Mearuras have we in Panguna?" Sikanai asked; his voice became sterner as he pulled open a drawer and took out a folder.

"*Umaudeaa, singnaing.* You know them; your forefathers' places," the younger fellow answered hesitantly.

Sikanai skimmed through his papers, picked what he wanted and stapled four pages together and handed them to the pair.

"*Kokore namono e. Mearura narii* ... but, you people keep

coming up with proposal after proposal on the same issue," Sikanai said as a peal of thunder echoed somewhere towards the east.

Oh, he - bureaucratic Sikanai - hated to be like that thunder which strikes and engages rudely with people but he had been continuously frustrated by so many opportunists trying to use the Bougainville crisis to build fortunes.

"Sorry men" he consoled," that paper passed through this office last year and now you come in with this." His eyes were fixed on the new proposal; as were the two clients on the old proposal.

Nobody uttered a word for a few minutes.

Pushing aside his fury and as calm as before Sikanai asked. "Who are the chiefs Karoro of Kokore and Taneavi of Mearura?"

The pair eyed each other. The older one had his head lowered as if in search of something. Then he took a deep breath and said, "*Te Karoro ning* and this is Taneavi." He pointed at himself and then the younger man as he sighed. He looked relieved.

"But we, or I personally, weren't involved in writing this," Taneavi pleaded like a child to a father. "Someone falsely signed my signature," He got a biro from his shirt pocket and signed a blank sheet of paper on the table and showed it to Sikanai. "Some idiots did this," he concluded with a frown.

Sikanai was now a detective investigating a crime as well as a bureaucrat in public office. He kept silent and listened attentively to the pair. He guessed that Karoro was involved in the old proposal. He stared and smiled at him, intermittently asking, "What do you, Karoro, think, about this?" The man just smiled guiltily, showing off his black teeth partitioned by a purple tongue – the impact of smoking and chewing areca nut for years.

"You know, my two brothers," Sikanai gently preached, trying to efface the tense feeling in the room, "we are turning Bougainville into *an Ameai* country'. We go from office to office, pestering; give me this and give me that, instead of making things possible ourselves."

"I really admire the words of that American leader, John F Kennedy; he said that, 'it is not so much what your country can do for you, but what you can do for your country'. If Bougainville could live along those lines we would have been a better-off place long ago." He paused as a sudden gust of wind blew the curtain towards the ceiling.

"The first proposal was paid for, I am sure," Sikanai said, after a pause. "What do you think, Karoro? You are so quiet." He chuckled and stared at the window waiting for Karoro to speak.

Sikanai knew that Karoro had been involved in the original proposal and that funding was released but that no reconciliation took place. Instead Duamei - Taneavi's own cousin; his favourite in their family - bought himself luxuries worth ten thousand kina.

He also knew that for a while, Karoro ceased frequenting Buka as before because a treasury officer was trying to catch him for the acquittals not done. They were waiting for him out there.

"You know," Karoro began, carefully, "that Duamei misused all that money. The officers in Buka are still waiting for acquittals.

"You two bastards," Taneavi interrupted. "That's why you never talk to each other, lately." He was chuckling.

"We had an argument at Panguna," Karoro continued "but I was no match for him. Duamei is just like his father, a talking puissant. I decided to befriend Taneavi, you know, because of the seriousness of the matter." He paused.

"So you two forged my signature?" Taneavi asked.

"Yes, that Duamei," answered Karoro.

Taneavi quietly mumbled: "Bastard; *piaarabaing.*"

"This problem," Karoro said, "must not get out of

control, dear God."

Bureaucratic Sikanai was listening, lazily. Once he thought about interrupting and telling them what they had been saying about crooks and pot bellies when he arrived; that was actually what they were themselves, but he decided not to for his own reasons. He stared at his watch, it was ten o'clock. Then, he looked at them and smiled.

"You will not secure more funding," he explained, "unless proper acquittals are handed in for the last grant." Karoro looked lost.

Sikanai thought for a moment and then told them, "I knew a lot of that Duamei; during the elections - the ABG elections - he was a very problematic person. He made claim after claim and complaint after complaint to me - he is a great opportunist."

"Bastard," Taneavi puffed.

"Beside," Sikanai said, clearing his voice, "your attempt to secure new funding for the same thing is stealing. Stealing from whom you may wonder? It is from those very Bougainvilleans you claim to serve."

"Okay, *te-a-te*, tampara," Taneavi said, standing to leave, "we'll just try sorting out these issues at home and see if we can come to terms with Duamei."

"*E, tampara bereaing*," Sikanai farewell them and they both walked out through the door wondering what to do next.

"Oh, to hell with independence Bougainville; we fought for it but now we are not sweating our guts out for it," Sikanai said to himself resting his head on the table with his eyes closed. He felt feverish. "How can we make it, dear God, by pestering ourselves?"

He knew the Bougainville way; the situation he had gone through today with these two fellows was disastrous for the Bougainville government. Feeling left out people turn to violence. That Taneavi could, by chance, come back and drive away with an administration car or burn down one of the offices. Who would bring him to justice then?

The police wouldn't be able to arrest him because of the barricades and guns. The would-be culprit would escape the law like everybody else. This was post-war Bougainville; an island with freedom fighters like dirty Duamei. Was he – Duamei - a fighter for freedom or a fighter for corruption?

His telephone rang, but he ignored it; quite fed up he left for an early lunch.

He was relieved. Outside the day was fine. The sky was azure, the breeze so cool and the mountains absolutely green. "What a beautiful and innocent island?" he murmured with a laugh, "but full of foolish and irresponsible islanders that I help protect."

He went off in the direction of the shopping centre, pacing slowly and taciturn.

Bani pininangka –penis sucker.
Mata ne –good morning.
Tampara –good day.
Areke e anangka – how are you (to more than two persons).
Anangka – hey (to more than one person).
Era – hey (to one person).
Umaudeaa – not many.
Singnaing – remains the same.
Namono e – only one.
Narii – same.
Te Karoro ning – I am Karoro.
Ameai– give it to me.
Piaarabaing – ought to masturbate his penis.
Te-a-te – okay.
Bereaing – you can go (dismissal).

8
THE CENTENARY VOYAGE

Akora was a grade 11 student at Hutjena Secondary School. His slim build and weakling-like posture had many of his school mates concluding that as an explanation for his easy-going attitude to life. But when he felt like slopping over the brim of his self-contained world it was hard to understand the new side of his personality.

Nobody, not even his own folks from Kieta, knew whether he had a Buka girl friend or not. It was hard to squeeze out his secrets - he was too stolid. But the rumour in the air was hard for him to deny. He was spotted in the dark hours with a certain Haku girl from Grade 9 in the brown classroom next to his own. He travelled to places that most Kietas feared. For his dreams and him nothing could come between.

The year 2001 was the hundredth year since Catholicism had landed in Bougainville. Jubilee celebration talks infiltrated every conversation in the school. Akora, although a Catholic and often attracted by the jubilee-related radio jingles, kept aloof for his own reasons.

Easterly and sea originating gusts of wind swept through the Hutjena Government Compound continuously harassing his reading. Intermittently, when the wind - with its ingrained cruelty - pitied him and abated, the loud sound of the singing by the practicing student choir in the mess hall took its turn to disturb his concentration.

"*Hey, Tebu, ol wokim wanem long mess?*" he asked his bunk mate making his ingress to Dorm 17.

"*Aung*, they are Catholics," Tebu answered, "practicing the centenary song. They'll be leaving on Thursday by ship for Tunuru in Kieta. Brother Joe from Hahela is conducting them."

Akora followed his mate into the dormitory and they sat lost in thought.

"*Sans, mi lukim peles pinis*," Akora said, boastfully as he turned to a new page in the novel that he was reading, *Things Fall Apart* by the Nigerian author, Chinua Achebe.

"No. Aung, they are saying that only the ones involved in the rehearsals are going," a boy grooming himself in his bunk said with a laugh.

Akora, with his mind concentrated on the book, absent-mindedly joked, "Sir, those nice voices and that *pesmeri*[4] conductor, if they happen to leave me here, they'll never get into Heaven. As for me, I'll be there with a carton of beer to party with my Lord. You know; I'll tell Him, Jesus, let's go back to the Cana days." They all laughed at the silly joke.

Days went by like the water in a river that has no resort to holidays. All the Kietas looked forward to a trip home in their centenary attire, if only to regain the smell of their so-missed home. From his distance Akora also shared with them that desire; that longing to be home.

Thursday found Akora very early in the dust and salt scented Buka township. Along the limestone gravel-covered streets Kietas wandered everywhere aimlessly. "So, you see, so many Kietas hiding in different corners of Buka island," he said to his friend and classmate, Barapanung.

"*Masikara, era*," Barapanung snuffled in the cloud of dust dragged along by a passing truck. "Many of them have never even felt a fine church pew even once." He paused to cross the road for the market, and then added, "Tonight, they'll all pack aboard the MV *Sankamap* for the joy of being seen in Tunuru as a bunch of faithful Catholics."

Akora reluctantly chuckled, "Aung, and what about us trying to get on board, have we any desire for fellowship with the church?"

"Always, we are." They laughed and entered the market.

Across the mighty and tenacious (if you fall into it) Buka Passage, the church chartered vessel was resting idly at Kokopau wharf, patiently waiting for the Tarlena Secondary School students and others to embark.

In the background of the growing Kokopau station the coconut palms lining the high ridge above were swaying in the wind with absolute fidelity. Just like Buka, trails of dust were marking the whereabouts of moving vehicles.

At the northern entrance of Buka Passage, just outside Iata village, gulls fished in the glare of the setting sun on a calm sea besmirched by the pure whiteness of the remnants of crushing mighty waves in the area believed to be the spot where the flowing passage water meets the immobile ocean.

The take-off horn of the ship blared at half five toppling those twang-like piercing sounds of the few motor boats ferrying across the passage through its undulations and bulging waves. "Era, otherwise that thing leaves us here," complained Akora, his eyes staring at the black diesel fumes emanating from the ship's funnel in the distance.

The boys were intrigued and tucked into the last contents of their food parcels before dashing out of the market. "That ship must be coming here," Barapanung reasoned. As they wondered the school truck appeared in front of them. "There, you see, the students are here. They will not be crossing the passage for the ship is coming to this side."

As they approached the wharf, the ship was there slowly engaging itself.

"*Anangka, de are kuada remang?*" a *wantok* straying near the port gate asked them. "Students are inside the gate, are you two going with them? Will you be on the ship?"

"No, we are only going to the bank's ATM," they lied. "Not interested in Kieta girls; the Buka one's are getting sweeter every day, you know."

This was Akora's way of answering questions from strangers. He loved short, cryptic answers where the enquirer must work out the rest in his own mind.

A good number of the choir students called to them as they walked under the street lamps but they ignored them, pretending not to be interested in being homeward bound.

They headed towards the bank and sat there watching the mass of people sorting out their travel papers. Later on they moved under the mango tree in front of the port's main entry gate, to Akora a handy site to keep an eye on developments.

The shrilling crickets annoyed them but they remained there calculating what steps they needed to take; one thing hindering them was the fact that neither had K15 to pay for the voyage to Kieta. Akora, however, had a plan.

"We'll go in there, together," Akora told his partner, "as we reach the money collector, I will send you back. That will give me time to play games with the cash-man, his receipt-boy and the person in the queue with me. Understood?"

"Yes!"

Strong gusts of wind were blowing litter everywhere. Leaves from the mango tree rained down on them. There were no twinkling stars high in the sky, just the powerful flash of lightning and the sound of thunder to the north. In the chilly air the boys marched towards the ship.

As they jostled through the crowd, an announcement was made, "All Hutjena students listen carefully as we read your names; when you hear your name cross the gang way. If your name is not called, you will have to pay K15 for a ticket."

As the list was read, the students snuggled into the floating house of the ship while the no-names began paying cash to Brother Joe, whose bald head, to Akora's amusement, glistened in the bright lighting of the ship. The boys approached him.

"And you two? *Painim wanem, maski lo bihainim ol meri*," Brother Joe, laughed. "Who is giving me K15?"

Akora watched Brother Joe write the receipts while the other brother, whom he was not sure about, collected the cash. Beside them, stood a couple of huge and aggressive looking security guards; the gangway was manned by them too.

"I will pay you," Akora said. "Barapanung just came to see me off." As an afterthought, he added, "Hey, Barapanung, my bag is there under the mango tree; go and fetch it."

"What were you doing under the mango tree?" Brother Joe asked, with a giggle.

"Just write me a receipt," Akora told him. Looking at the woman in the queue behind him he said, "Hey, woman pay money to the cashier and this Brother will write you the receipt."

"Have you paid too?" Brother Joe asked him.

"You write my receipt and keep it there and I'll go and pay; you'd better write this woman her receipt as well."

Brother Joe did just that and Akora moved over to the cash collector and handed him some areca-nut and started a conversation. They chatted like old friends, occasionally getting the receipt-man involved. When he thought he had them in his trap he would go back to Brother Joe for his receipt and he was sure he wouldn't hesitate to hand it to him since he had been with the cash-man for some minutes. The timing was perfect and he presented himself to Brother Joe, again.

"My receipt, please?" he asked, confidently.

"Here you are, and safe trip, my *pamuk* boy."

As planned, Akora boarded the ship and then walked to the bow area and handed the ticket to Barapanung, who was, after a few minutes, safe on board beside his partner. They relaxed and looked forward to the voyage ahead.

All this was done under the brewing storm. Then came the mooring lines, followed by the gearing up of the ship's engine, which felt like an earth tremor to Akora.

The ship steamed towards the open sea and Kieta in pitch darkness, unsteadily hustling against the tormenting winds and gigantic waves.

Waves as high as Mount Takuang attacked the ship continuously, causing stifling discomfort for poor Akora who now thought of nothing but sea sickness. "We are entering the mouth of a devil storm, boy," Akora told Barapanung as they sat on the wet coaming canvas. "Let's go into one of the cabins."

Nobody was interested in exploring the warmness of the cabin with the waves hammering the vessel. Akora held tightly onto the canvas seam even though some stability had been gained and the floating house was churning on through the tempestuous sea. Fear gripped him yet.

To further add to their displeasure rain poured down in a torrent in collaboration with the cruelly rollicking wind hissing in the struts. Nobody was stable: people stood and then sat and uttered complaints or just wandered about, hands clutching at anything for balance - not even taking the chance to glimpse at the storm outside.

Akora lay prone on a bed offered to him by an old friend, Asino a student from Tarlena. He was sick in the belly. "You know, I felt awkward taking up this bed when other people needed it," Asino boasted in a distant murmur; but pain was permeating his bravado. "You are lucky." The ship quaked and he too was dangling over the bed vomiting with heavy gasps. Somewhere a child was wailing in gulps too.

With his chin resting on his wrist Akora painfully scanned the room. Everywhere people vomited onto the metal floor. A few with a little strength left staggered outside but returned wet all over from the sea spray and rain. Occasionally people bumped into the rails or bed frames as the vessel jerked uncontrollably.

As he laid in discomfort, Akora chided himself for

taking this journey. "Why did I take up this voyage," he murmured. The thought of jumping overboard momentarily occurred to him but he dismissed it quickly. "Get lost, he said." He prayed with the woman next to him. As he meditated he kept his eyes on his female neighbour. She was mumbling in dulcet tones with a rosary resting in her palms.

He initially eyed her cynically but then admonished himself. She was beautiful, like every student from Tarlena, especially now with that frightened look. Her hair was neatly braided and a white t-shirt covered her agile body.

Just then, a giant of a wave struck. The churning of the ship's engine wavered. The clock on the wall that was reading midnight was suddenly not there anymore. The ship jerked, bounced and then jerked again and again. Impetuous was its lurching.

Akora was not within his senses. In the darkness he attempted desperately to get to his feet but to no avail. He tried to scream but not a sound was uttered as the whole mass of the rosary girl, Jacklyn, was stuck to him. Her cheek blocked his mouth from calling while her bare thighs were all tangled up with his.

The smell of strong perfume overwhelmed him. Her warmth was erotic and liberating from the defiant storm outside. They both - now having each other for comfort-considered the dangers outside as a soothing lullaby for them - two desperate lovers.

Akora ran his palm down her smooth back and hesitantly under her panties. He began caressing her buttocks to no objection.

The darkness was prolonged due to some mechanical mischief in the ship's engine. With that blessing he straddled her and they made love as the terrified people around them, mindful only of their own survival, ignored them.

The morning sun caught them in separate beds as the ship slowly made its way into Loloho wharf. They eyed each other with affection and talked about the new place before them. Jacklyn was taken by the rugged mountains and giant boulders that reached high into the skies of Kieta and her brown eyes were wide.

White seagulls soared high in welcome. The green mountains and rolling hills, mottled here and there by huge white galip nut tree trunks, were magnificent to the Petats Island girl.

The ship docked carefully against the wharf and the lovers walked down the gangway laughing to themselves and discussing what had crept into their world.

"Aung, from which corner of Kieta do you come from?" Jacklyn asked shyly as they strolled in front of a bunch of curious onlookers.

"Panguna is where you belong, darling."

"*Em orait tasol,*" she said proudly and hugged him before the dozens of wondering eyes.

Tebu, ol wokim wanem long mess? - what's going on in the mess?
Aung - hey!
Mi lukim peles pinis - already, I am at home!
Masikara, era - yes (agreement).
Pes-meri – womaniser.
Anangka, de are kuada remang? - where are you running to?
Wantok - person one is sharing the same language with.
Painim wanem, maski lo bihainim ol meri - what are you after, stop running after women.
Pamuk – promiscuous.
Em orait tasol - it's okay.

9

THE MOON WALK

The Bougainville crisis brought so many positive changes into the lives of the islanders. For example, people were now moving freely without the fear of the red skinned rascals that dwelled in the squatter settlements and ambushed people on the outskirts of Arawa.

Perfect was the wind of change. Nights were the same as the daytimes - secure - because everyone under the sun was jet black - a Bougainvillean.

But this freedom was short lived. It dawned like the daybreak and was swiftly washed away by anarchy. The self-styled rule of the Bougainville Revolutionary Army quickly divided free Bougainville. In just a matter of months, lives - those Bougainvillean lives - were in boiling water.

Those troubled Bougainvilleans re-invited the infidel redskins back. The government soldiers added their contribution, neither good nor bad, to the chaos. So the island was truly a land of suffering. Dreams were shattered

Black Ma knew it all; normalcy was unimaginable. Freedom was just an illusion. Her beloved husband, a redskin, had been killed by her kinsmen – the so-called freedom fighters. This gave her independence, she was alone with absolute power, to make decisions to bring about change upon her growing five children - now fatherless in this land they loved the most.

Black Ma was a well-built woman with tight curly blonde hair. Her temperament was often dictated by circumstances. Good times were good times and vice-versa. She scolded loafers. At the top of her voice she would scream, "Go to your fathers and mothers, you sick in the head. You roam here and there as if a snake is rotting in your home." So wanderers never intruded on her abode, unnecessarily.

However, since the killing of the family's father, Pomong hamlet was in a desolate situation. Then Black Ma and her children entertained a new set of friends. These were the infiltrators who went in and out of the government controlled area of Arawa at random. Nobody suspected them of anything untoward. The whole village of Kupe knew that they were innocent or not that type.

In their kindness and pity for the victimized family, Simaraka and his wife revealed themselves one day.

"You know, Black Ma," Simaraka began, "it's worthwhile for your children to see their papa's homeland. They can care for them there, too. They are growing old and very much need to go to school. I can be of help in regard to the Papua New Guinea Defence Force and the Resistance Fighters out there."

Black Ma and her first born son, Dangkiroi, were open mouthed. "So...you mean you go there, unnoticed, Simaraka?" Black Ma said with a pout and shrug as Sinu, Simaraka's wife gave a broad smile.

"Yes, aunty we do," Sinu answered, "we go down to the Arawa and Pavaire defence force camps bringing them vegetables. In return they give us tin fish and so on."

"Gracious Jesus," Black Ma laughed, "you two culprits - you should have died, instead of my husband."

"You see, Black Ma," Simaraka came in patting Dangkiroi on the right shoulder, "this boy needs schooling just like the rest of the children."

"The authorities at Arawa have said the schools there will open once the Papua New Guinea Defence Force fully secure the edges of the township," Sinu added.

Standing up and walking towards the fireplace to light his pipe, Simaraka concluded, "What do you think ma? I am taking my children there once the schools open."

Simaraka and his woman left. They were gone - these betrayers of Bougainville. Black Ma was left in a storm of thought: the government care centres and education were both tangled up and couldn't be easily separated. Education was worth thinking about but the care centres were a problematic puzzle.

Previously the BRA men said life in the government controlled areas was like hell. The army killed people at will. Women were raped and the dead were dumped in the sea. The bush boys were painting this picture to keep people on their side of the rope. The infiltrators were now painting a different picture.

People in the government care centres, according to the likes of Simaraka, had free rations, clothing and freedom to travel out of the area in government chartered ships and planes. This was freedom, the sort Black Ma desired. There was education, in those army guarded camps. Children like Black Ma's, were in school there, while here in this horrid bush hideout the children had never heard a single word in the white men's language.

Black Ma had been a high school student but she hadn't completed her education when she eloped with her husband. She had been praying hard to God that her children could carry-on from where she left. Off. She was fixed and she was determined for a moon walk to Arawa in search of freedom and education for the future Bougainvilleans.

Very early one morning Dangkiroi, woke up very early ready to go out hunting bats. His mother caught him sneaking out. "Son, go to Tangkukovi right away and fetch your uncle Simaraka."

"*Aping ko?*"

"You will go collecting dry coconut for *tama-tama* at Bakabori. That's why." His mother lied.

When Dangkiroi and Simaraka came back, Black Ma was busy at the fireplace with the preparation of breakfast for her children. The smoke from the kitchen wouldn't allow her fresh air to breath and she dashed out with tears forming in her eyes.

"E, so you are here, so early," she coughed for fresh

air.

Simaraka just chuckled in wonder. He was curious about why his relative should call him so very early in the morning. He was reluctant to ask but his words just slipped out. "What was this call for mama?"

Black Ma was back in the kitchen. "Well...well my mind is determined; I am going to Arawa with my children. So I am ordering you and Dangkiroi to spy out the Bakabori trail that leads into Topinang for me. Clear up little bushes and so on."

"Thank you, *ani*," Simaraka was relieved of his wondering. "I told your *barau* Andrew in Arawa, that his sister Black Ma would soon join him there. It wasn't a mistake."

"So, you went to Arawa, ape," Black Ma shrugged, and came back out of the kitchen.

"No, not at Arawa but Pavaire," Simaraka corrected, "He came there looking for areca nuts. He has become a great chewer."

After breakfast, Simaraka lead his company, Dangkiroi and his younger brother, Mirongko on their reconnaissance walk. The cool mountain breeze kept the gang fresh under the burning heat of the sun. No sweat to bother. Slings by the brothers propelled stones here and there often missing the terrified birds that left instantly for safety.

Around boulders they went. A few creeks cooled them further before arriving at Siriang a deserted hamlet and they were lost. "From here which way does it go?" Simaraka asked, since he'd never followed this trail.

The brothers had walked this track many times before but the over grown bushes confused them a little. Dangkiroi looked everywhere.

"There, I think underneath that *karikau* tree is where we usually walk to Topinang."

He was right. People from the hideouts were still using the Topinang trail to go to Bakabori, skirting the sides, and avoiding the once beautiful lawns of Siriang.

In a matter of minutes the party reached an observation point - Namuna. This is a ridge with its base on the Crown Prince Range dividing Bovong and Dangkua valleys. It is immaculately pinnacled by gigantic boulders, notably Biirikobiriko and the Orempi chain of boulders that overlook Arawa from the south-west.

In the distance Pavaire village looked innocent but she housed gunmen - armed to the teeth - who long to see blood spilled. From her womb, men came into the valleys of Dangkua and Bovong to kill. To go there was to tempt fate.

The Dangkua valley was in a peaceful silence. Lifelessly mourning the loss of a son recently killed at Pavaire on a night raid.

"Okay you know the foot tracks leading to the main road very well. The Topinang men are in sorrow so ther is no problem," Simaraka said to the boys after his thoughts had accumulated. "When the time comes, walk where we have been and what you know. No new track boys."

Mirongko who had now been informed about his mother's plan laughed. "E, the difficult part is what we've already covered .From here to Pavaire is nothing." Everyone smiled and headed homewards.

"*Paapa* Simaraka will not be around for a while," Dangkiroi was saying as he carefully watched the manoeuvres of a lone robin in a guava tree outside their kitchen. "He said his decision is to avoid suspicion".

Black Ma was swift, "It's common sense. Was the trail clear?"

"Yes. As clear as that lawn of ours," Mirongko, who was fiddling with a catapult snapped in.

Black Ma and her two sons were in deep thought while the much younger girls: Amea, Tavo and Dome played kick-and-run joyfully laughing and shouting like some heavenly angels. Their voices echoed through the Konnaiang Gorge with the cool morning breeze.

The girls knew nothing. Even if they had listened attentively, their age would have denied them a clear picture of the gravity of what they were doing.

"Tomorrow we will go," Black Ma said and interest flared in the facial expressions of the elder children. They showed approval coloured by a little fear.

"We'll go through Kumpou hideout so our footprints will be quickly covered by the occupants there," she added. This was clever because, with children and belongings, their pace would be slow and they chanced falling prey to the BRA boys.

It was one of those nights, the Kieta's say the moon fools the cuscus in the forest. The moon rises at early dawn, the poor mammals thinking it is still the night, continue their search for fruits but suddenly discover themselves under the glare of the morning sun. They rush to hide and rest anywhere and are often caught by hunters who know it's a good time to hunt them.

Black Ma knew that because the people at Kupe would be out hunting the cuscus early it would be late before they realised she and her family were gone and raised the alarm.

When a cock crowed once in the far distance Black Ma was fully awake packing a parcel of roasted taro into her knapsack. A steel pot rattled in the sack as she further sorted her possessions. Her four children had their own little packs to carry. Dome, the last born of the family, was to be shouldered by the boys, through the eight hours it would take them to travel.

In the approaching dawn bats were crisscrossing the Pomong sky looking for suitable resting places as the fatherless family took off; their determined mother leading, followed by the muscular Mirongko with Dome calmly resting on his shoulders in wonder. Their silhouettes looked like troopers without guns.

As they walked in the coldest hours of the night their

bodies began warming. Clothes began sticking to their moist skin as they slowly began to climb the Western side of the Birareko hillock with their loads. They slowly descended into the Kumpou cluster of huts occupied by coastal refugees.

"Carefully," Black Ma cautioned," Don't stir up any attention, come this way."

As they passed the last hut Black Ma prayed loudly, "Thank you God of this sinful earth,". Tavo made the sign of the cross and her mother witnessed and appreciated it when she turned back to see her siblings.

Leaving Siriang behind, the family had to wade through a patch of grass heavy with dew. Amea cried disapproval. "This road is full of grass. I am getting wet, mama."

"Forget it daughter," Black Ma consoled. "You'll get dry later on."

"Era, you didn't want to follow us on Monday and clear this up," Dangkiroi laughed. Everyone chuckled quietly.

The once noisy village of Topinang was lifeless. Cocks cried in the dark Rocky Mountains in a westerly direction. Black Ma and her family carefully made their way through the ghost village. A few loose sheets of roofing iron clunked in the light wind that blew. A familiar car stood idle.

With Black Ma leading the way, full light caught the family at a place called Sietangking Junction. The road was now clear with PNGDF truck tyre marks clearly visible on the muddy earth. "We will slowly walk up to Pavaire," Black Ma told her children.

Cocoa trees swayed to the rhythm of the wind. The air was welcoming and Black Ma was burning with confidence about a safe walk to freedom.

The road to Pavaire was an hour's walk uphill. They caught glimpses of the mountain village when the line of cocoa and coconut trees permitted. As they moved up the slope the PNGDF camp came into view positioned right on the peak of Tarama boulder that lifts Pavaire so high.

And in that camp during the night, Soldier Brown, a Morobean, had had a dream. In his dream, he saw a short and well-built red skinned man telling him, 'My family is coming'.

So, in the morning he went out and was telling his story to a mate over a cup of coffee when Black Ma reached the edges of the village, though still out of sight of the camp.

As he sat talking, a hen and her chicks, about fifty metres away, cackled in fear and fled in all directions. Black Ma and her siblings appeared and bravely sauntered across the mowed lawn towards the main bunker that was occupied by Soldier Brown.

"What was I telling you, mate, there's the family," he whispered to his comrade who agreed with him and went to heat up the camp kettle. Word diffused through the camp, and soldiers flocked in to greet the new arrivals.

"*Sindaun, sindaun na malolo ol pikinini*," Soldier Brown, ushered them to seats. "The soldiers are preparing some food for you."

Over breakfast, Soldier Brown related his story to the family. The red skinned man's appearance in his dream really matched the late father of this fatherless family. He had just recently been murdered by the Bougainville Revolutionary Army for crossing the no-man's land from West New Britain Province to Kupe village for his deep love of his Bougainvillean family.

"*Sori stret, ol pikinini*," Soldier Brown, said blinking automatically to fight off his tears, "When I saw these mixed raced children, I knew my dream was real."

From the end of the camp came a soldier carrying a huge machine gun with its necklace of bullet hanging around his neck and down his back. The children curiously eyed him.

"Yeah, children, we called the soldiers down in Arawa and they are coming to fetch you." As he passed the little girls were training their taste buds on the biscuits they knew nothing about, he added, "*Hamamas na stap, bai iron car blong army kam kisim yupla.*"

For Black Ma the air was free here. Life was something to be proud of once again after all that she endured in the mountains of Kupe. Not that, it was over, but here, there was a room for change through education for her poor fatherless children.

Black Ma eyed the fruits of her love, from the first to the last as warm tears freely trickled down her cheeks.

Aping ko - why?
Tama-tama - a Kieta food (pudding) made from food mashed in a mortar and fried in coconut oil.
Karikau - Malay Apple.
Papa — uncle.
Sindaun, sindaun na malolo ol pikinini - take a seat and rest, children.
Sori stret, ol pikinini - very sad for the kids.
Hamamas na stap, bai iron car blong army kam kisim yupla - keep calm, an armoured car is coming to fetch you.

10
KAMARI NANKA

The chopper landed in the heart of the landing square sweeping off a storm of spiralling dust. A dozen metres away the elephant grass that surrounded the Turiboiru PNGDF care centre camp was laid flat on the ground in fear of the spinning rotors.

"We had an hour of fire exchange, yesterday," Nukuitu, a red eyed resistance commander told the new Papua New Guinea Defence Force commander. 'They came hot for us and went away.'

"Did they get anyone?" the commander asked.

"No, but it was the worst screwing ever."

Just by his look, the commander was from the highlands of Papua New Guinea. The people whom the Kietas of Bougainville; refer to as, 'kau'mintung po'nanka' or 'legs with intestine'. This is because they have very large calves with prominent veins. And his build was great. He was tall and compared to him Nukuitu, the Bougainvillean, was just a little child.

The commander stood up and went for a little stroll around the camp. He was amazed by the number of thatched huts across the little drop. Just a stone-throw away was the first hut. It was walled by government supplied blue canvas.

Every dawn, in these homesteads, you had to have your chats with your various gods quickly for the home guards were not concerned about your deities, they just came waking you to cut grass till midday.

In the distance, but not far enough to be too safe from a bullet was Taunu - Turiboiru's sister camp. With the dusty airstrip alongside it the camp suffers from dust storms created by army planes and so on. Thus, everywhere there were coughing children playing and acting soldiers in action, telling the world that they were victims of the war situation.

Sometimes gossip floats through the air of these care centres that a particular couple have being interrupted making love by these carefree children engaged in their games of hide-and-seek.

The space between the camps is covered with swaying elephant grass and criss-crossed by gullies that meet the Loruru river in the westward forest.

A gravel road runs through this land. From the north comes another road that links the latter to the no-man's land that runs south to Taunu. All fear this land as the rebels regularly set ambushes there.

Early the next morning the commander, now christened Fatnose, because of his large nose, woke early in the dawn with the cock and marched into the civilian Bougainvillean cook's hut. The cook was still snoring away.

"Hey you bastard, you're supposed to be cooking," he roared at the chef. "You what, a fat lady? Fuckin' *yu, go kuk*." The cook was following the old rules, though he knew the Bible passage that reads: 'The old has gone and the new has come.'

With a new person you have to apply new rules. Without time to wash and clean his teeth to subdue his halitosis, he got the fire crackling under the black camp teapot.

"Thank you," the commander exulted him, "you Bougainvilleans have sweet hands, especially your black girls. You must arrange one for me."

He watched as a gang of teenage girls at the fringe of the camp perimeter strolled past with the sun reflected on their smooth skin.

"E, there they go again. The sun is also romantically inclined to them," he told himself as he ran his tongue along the cup rim with his mind full of kissing scenes.

"Girls here are unique," he said to his batman, "they are black, soft and cunning. What word can I use to describe their pubes?" They laughed. As an afterthought, he added: "Our girls grow wrinkle too early whilst a Buin girl is still going strong, even with five children. For exhausting myself fighting for them, I need to rape one soon; in front of her parents."

The cup of coffee in his hand was forgotten while his mind was clouded with a dozen girls making love to him, a middle aged Eastern Highlander. Though he was a father of three back in his own country, he believed it was worthwhile in Bougainville tasting a black woman.

As he drifted through his fantasy an uproar of gunfire went off somewhere to the north. He spilled his coffee on his naked left thigh and it burned like fire.

"Cover up, you bastards!" he shouted as he dashed into the bunker.

"Those fuckin waterproof rebels again," Jimmy the batman said as they watched a pillar of smoke rising into the air. "You see, another hut belonging to the people who love Papua New Guinea is down to ashes again. The bushmen attack us with kerosene."

When the contact ceased the commander ordered troops out to inspect the damage. They maneuvered past eyes that were glaring at them as if to say, 'What are you looking at us for? The ones you are looking for are beyond the perimeters of this camp.'

Somewhere amongst the mass of terrified people, Private Robin spotted a familiar girl flat on the ground, as they moved towards the battle front. Her conical breasts were flattened on her chest. He stared at her, thinking the gun he held in hand gave him the right to stare, but angry eyes scared him away.

The rebels were already gone; in the bush they were laughing and saying what are these cowards, then, doing in the middle of us? The people often wonder why.

"Two brave fighters are down," Nukuitu snarled and

cursed the BRA men.

"From where, did they shoot?" someone asked him.

"The elephant grass."

Two resistant fighters were on the ground dead. Flies orbited around them as the women folk wailed over their lost children.

"Our brothers will every day slaughter us," cried old Kebau, in his own language to keep the *ivitu* soldiers from understanding, "We are just a shield for these pests. Damn bastards! A country's army here for nothing; they are just security guards deployed here on a mission beyond their knowledge."

Someone added: "You see them; they are here while our own resistance fighters track the killers into the bush. Better for them to be in the bush where the BRA will skin them alive, instead of just acting like commandoes in front of our girls."

Later in the afternoon, the resistant fighters returned with casualties.

"Two men have being lost and three wounded. Three issued rifles gone to the bushmen," a PNGDF soldier reported to the commander.

"These idiots must have given those guns to their brothers and are telling lies," Fatnose said as he ordered a soldier to call Loloho for a chopper to evacuate the wounded.

An enormous colony of nimbus piled in the north-east as the buzzing sound of the flying machine made for the camp. Eyes were skimming the clouds competing to see who would be the first to see the helicopter.

"Now you see those clouds there, the rebels under them are forcing their wives onto their beds for sex," Fatnose said to Minsipi, one of the resistance fighters, as they stood waiting for the chopper.

"Yes, they are," Minsipi snapped and walked away.

The chopper, picked up her cargo and left for Buka and the people stood watching her fading towards Siwai.

The evening was fine. The sun was on the western horizon tired and sleepy. Far inland the Deuro Range was wet but clear. Birds were high; warming up and hunting for the last meal of wild fruits and insects. But the care centre was silent, it was in mourning and fear. Why do Bougainvilleans kill each other? The Kietas who started it should tell us. But they to, are killing each other?

"Tomorrow, they'll bury the men," said Major Mosi, who oversaw the care centre, "so please take part in the funeral rituals. Many girls will be there; women here too need money which their men cannot provide them. So waste no money."

This did not interest Fatnose very much. "Funerals are where boys and girls screw most of the time," he said, sounding like a tired man. "These Bougainvilleans are too nasty for me. So many things are now in my head. Who are we fighting?"

"Why do you say this chief?" the batman asked.

"Go back home and fuck your Sepik girl, my partner," The commander said and laid down to sleep.

Major Mosi was listening from his bed to all the conversation. "In the night a bullet can give you the kissogram. Our government's 'divide and conquer' is not working out."

The night was cold and clear with the moon high in the sky. It showed clearly the scars that survived from wounds it had sustained when it was attacked by birds in the Widoi Mountains behind Kieta. But Fatnose could not sleep, so he went outside.

Seated on a stool he stared into the dark, wondering what tomorrow could bring. Fire flies wandered here and there in the dark without bothering him. He sneezed, stood up and strolled into the open as a bat released its grip from a coconut frond and left.

Somewhere in the dark a stereo was playing local songs. Fatnose thought it was the sentry but it wasn't, it came from the Mekeo Private Robin's corner.

"Big ball, didn't you hear about the killings?" the commander shouted, "What will the people say to me and you? They won't tell us anything, but just pick up your gun, shoot you and off into the jungle they go."

The music went off without hesitation followed by a weak echo of gunfire somewhere in the northern jungles. The rebels were celebrating for their successes for the day just gone by.

Was killing a human being worth jubilation? For Bougainvilleans, it could be so because they are striving for their rights. And for PNG, which is actually in the wrong place in this Pacific-Africa? Fatnose was lost to his questions.

A cool breeze engulfed Fatnose as a straying firefly orbited him. 'What do you want?' he asked the insect as he approached the sentry. The distant chorus of traditional funeral songs was sweeping through the camp loudly keeping awake every one.

"What do you think of those songs?" a sentry asked, as he welcomed him.

"They are best. Bougainville is best, just like the rest of her sister islands in the Solomons."

Nobody talked but kept silent, as if consuming the contents of the commander's statement word by word.

At dawn Major Mosi was interrupted making love to a Buin girl in his dirtiest dream since arriving in Bougainville by the blasts of mortar shells. He eagerly rummaged his bed but nowhere was the girl.

"Fuckin' shells, kiss your operator's grubby arse," he cursed after the reality got to him.

As the burial went on the mortar platoon kept busy all morning, shelling the northern belts that were infested by the BRA in preparation for the operation to 'eliminate' the regular attacks and infiltrations into the care centre. But Fatnose had doubts: this is their home, what is meant by 'elimination' anyway?

Far inland, the resultant explosions were tremendous. A myriad of echoes swept across the plains. Scared were those innocent hearts; even nature wept in the sky, there was no life.

It was a busiest day, for the occupying forces. A company just flown in from Kieta was preparing alongside their friends, the pro-PNG resistant groups. Private Robin was reassembling his M16 and at the same time telling Minsipi, his tales with the rifle in hand.

"This brat once jammed as I was about to shoot down a BRA man upstream in the Bovo River," he said as he nodded his head. "The bastard got a lucky escape after sending a private from Delta Company to heaven."

"Why didn't the others get him?" Minsipi asked.

"Those pricks were shocked and stood there watching like boles. But thank heaven; the bullets missed their big heads."

Minsipi just chuckled, helping himself to more bullets. "Years of training and still you get shocked by terror." Both men just laughed at that.

Though prepared for the operation, Jimmy the batman, kept his distance, the whole day. Hardly, was he seen on the outside but remained in his bed thinking about home. Only once in a while did he pop up to the orders from the commander. Because of such commitment to duty, his mates often thought of him as a chip off the old block back home.

Mosi watched him enter the dining area and took a seat next to him. "Good afternoon brother. Are you prepared?"

"Yes brother, going to put my best foot forward. And what about you soldier?" The batman turned to face his mate who seemed to be preoccupied by something.

"I am thinking about my wife?" Mosi said, swallowing a spoon of steaming rice.

"Why?"

"Well, I don't know whether I'll end up dead or alive."

Mosi's voice began trembling. Tears rolled down his cheeks, freely. To this Jimmy was surprised because this fellow always preached about loyalty and bravery in the army. Anyway, people do change when faced with contrasting circumstances. So, he just sat there waiting for his friend to relieve himself.

"Brother, we'll be all right," Jimmy advised. "You are not alone; we are all suffering that same pain."

The night was very long for Jimmy. His mind was like a pendulum, moving back and forth. He was visiting his family in Kerema - chatting with them - and then back on Bougainville facing a BRA man who is rushing at him to have him dead.

"Wake up, men," someone at the sentry post shouted. "Take-off hour and where is that commander, still sleeping like a fat lady?" The voice of the sentry was more like a duty teacher in a high school.

The commander jumped out of his bed, shouting, "Get moving. Move it!" without realizing that he was the last to disengage from his mattress.

"Fuckin' you," someone scolded him.

Realizing that he was the last to leave the 'cool lady' he kept silent for he knew he had failed in his duty and if he kept talking he would be manhandled to the ground.

Major Mosi glanced at his wrist watch; it was 2 am as the troops forced their way through a massive cluster of flying insects to the main road. A wandering insect crashed into his neck and shocked him. "Lucky, and you are not a human being or we could sort this out with our fists," he told himself with a chuckle.

Soon the warmth of the morning sun poured on them in the thick undergrowth, off the north road.

"What is this river?" the commander asked Nukuitu.

"Loruru'" the resistant fighter said as he slowed his pace to decode the scout's gestures. As he did he spotted something?

The wilderness was so sweet. High in the trees, birds

sang morning songs. Somewhere nearby a hornbill, startled by the presence of human beings, left with very heavy flapping of its wings; followed by loud cackling of crows. All this made the commander anxious.

"Shit, you bastards!" Fatnose, warned nature, "get lost, you panty-less lunatics."

Far across a fallowed area - the length of a soccer pitch - a young hunter, with his catapult aimed at a noisy party of parrots was struggling to get a specific target. To Fatnose this was not an ordinary man but a hard core guerrilla fighter. He was probably not alone and as vulnerable as he looked.

"Company split," Fatnose instructed, "one half to the rear and strike and they will come running to us."

As the orders were passed through the lines the bushes behind the lone, bare chested hunter came into focus. There were men talking and smoke from a fire was visible as it crept under the shade of the canopy.

The scouts of the rear strike force led their men through a dense tangle clearing their way with their gun muzzles. They maneuvered cautiously; as insects shrilled and mosquitoes feasted on them in millions. But all they concentrated on was getting in place and killing this problem for PNG.

A falling dried leaf spun and brushed the point scout's helmet, passed down his belly, rested for a few seconds on this gun barrel and went on to the ground to rest. The scout eyed it suspiciously but then forced himself to forget it.

Suddenly, a flapping sound occurred and off into the air something went - a megapod. Behind it came an exhausted mongrel, but its quest to slaughter its prey bore no fruit. Here, ahead of him, were smells he had never come across before. He halted and sniffed the odours - they were new. The dog watched the scout.

"What is that?" the second scout asked through the tangle.

"That dog had me dead."

It was still there watching the scouts. But, slowly it secured its tail to its abdomen and to the men's alarm it gave an angry bark and dashed into the tangled growth.

In the distance, the irate dog never ceased howling. The echo travelled and shook the entire jungle world. The dog sat and was calling to the gods that the *ivitu* are here with us, trying to kill us in our own land.

"My god, that dog," Nukuitu cried.

Minsipi, who did not seem at all disturbed by this stood relaxed watching Nukuitu. "Don't be bothered by a naked puppy, man."

Someone in the midst of the targeted area, gave a shout for withdrawal; the dog was also pacified.

"Thanks Jesus," the point scout felt relief from his enveloping fear. He was an inmate walking to freedom.

The other troopers led by Fatnose crossed the cold Loruru and positioned themselves on the edge of the fallowed area. For, it was here that the enemy would come running to when attacked from the rear.

They waited silently in anticipation for the moment to squeeze the trigger. Every soldier longed to kill a Bougainvillean rebel for their country. They have caused Port Moresby so much trouble.

They waited, as the rear strike force struggled through a vast bamboo cluster. They came across evidence of human activity. Ahead, the land was getting higher so the soldiers moved more carefully so as not to be spotted.

To the left of the creeping government men and amidst impenetrable undergrowth, were their enemies.

Nande, the point scout of Sepik origin who was renowned for his tales of training with Australian soldiers sprang over a huge rotting log with deepening heart beats after catching something with his sharp ears. He brushed past a spiky pile of pandanus leaves that were hanging loose on their mother palm to get a clear view of the rebel position.

With sweat dripping down his face and veins clear on his face, he halted and gestured his second man forward.

A soft conversation was audible some fifty metres away under the thick undergrowth. Bluish fire smoke was also visible.

"They are here," the scouts concluded and ordered the men into position.

Overhead, a lone crow flapped its way through the shade of the canopy as Nukuitu took a few steps forward escorted by Minsipi.

A light wind, swept the jungle to life. Mosquitoes were like African swarms. In the distance, a branch cracked.

The wind must be mad, thought Nukuitu.

Cautiously, the soldiers moved forward in formation for attack. With his heart pounding, Nukuitu didn't mind who was minding the back, what he wanted was the blood that was there in front of him. There they were talking without knowing that death was creeping in silently.

The wind was still up and the shrubs were swaying in a leisurely manner. But Manu, a Morobean soldier serving his fifth year in the PNG Defence Force was hard hit by the mosquitoes. The parasites were trying their best to attack his neck, making him shake his head frequently. Over the numerous boles and bushes they harangued him till he saw something - who? A rebel! He moved in a jerk to his right.

"There!" he pointed! Shoot... shoot!" he ordered as he landed on the moist earth shooing away the army of mosquitos. The troops fired. Bullets had the leaves and tree branches falling like rain to the mother earth. Not a response came.

Firing, the troops moved forward. Reloading and firing they went towards the enemy that had cost them so much discomfort.

Minsipi, the end-man on the far left of the barrage and the first in front of the enemy, halted fire after hearing a radio playing. It was running a broadcast on environmental issues from Australia.

His heart pounded as he sought to identify a gap into which to escape and meet his kinsmen. He swore at the radio loudly, "Fuck you," and switched it off. It belonged to his cousin - another resistant fighter turned rebel.

On the other side Fatnose and his men were firing into the fallow area. It was clear that through this zone no being could cross without been spotted. Nothing, but fear was motivating this Australian trained army. Good for nothing pricks! They were, however, creating windows for the execution of his secret plan of serving his rebel kinsmen.

"Keep shooting," Fatnose ordered all sides. "These men are like ghosts, they can cross this way without you seeing them, boys "

Under the deafening blast of guns and grenades, Minsipi stood still watching the soldiers. They, without restraint, were wasting Australian ammunition on innocent plants. The bush boys had only one formula and that was: 'one shot equals one kill' and then off into the jungle.

As he stood lost in thought, a soldier kneeling before him was hit. He heard the piercing thud of a bullet breaking through human flesh, and was shocked. What if they - my very relatives - take me down and their supply of ammunition still with me?

The *ivitu* topped over on the ground struggling by reflex and thinking that he could still retain his precious life, but sadly he didn't make it. Minsipi just stared at the man, hopelessly.

"Heaven; or hell, my friend," Minsipi said, "It's up to you and God, at least he knows who you are, you bastard."

There was no one behind Minsipi and then, to his joy, his uncle Kepa appeared.

Minsipi signalled Kepa to come forward as he fired an agreed pattern of shots to indicate to the rebels their presence and exact position. They both watched Nukuitu come forward with two soldiers.

"Hey, that one is shot," Kepa said to Nukuitu and the two soldiers, who were surprised and halted fire in perplexity.

More soldiers came. They were shocked that one of their men was down without them even knowing from where the killer took his shot. Was he now selecting his next target they wondered. Out of anger, some of the men began shooting everywhere. On the other side, Fatnose, after a short radio briefing kept shooting the trees.

Men gathered around the dead man. Some were weeping for their comrade; others kept shooting, just to drive the fear out of their spines.

"It won't be long - ," Minsipi was instructing Kepa on the next step.

The sad gathering was taken by surprise! A sudden heavy round of gun fire came sweeping through the jungle. Missiles smashed rotting boles, tore through leaves and knocked down branches. Government men ran in all directions trying to save their lives.

Muzzle smoke crept in as a dreadlocked rebel stood up behind the smoke line and shouted angrily at the Redskins telling them to return to PNG and fuck their mothers.

A dozen soldiers were lost in confusion. Others sprinted off like wild pigs; crushing into giant boles, landing hard and then getting up and darting off again. Not a soldier was thinking of the weapon in his hand when the rebels - so determined for a kill - jumped forward firing. Some of the government men were heard screaming, 'mama,' as they headed for the fallow ground.

"Where are they shooting from?" a soldier with blood bubbling out of one of his eye sockets, shouted as he landed on the ground in front of a resistance fighter who just laughed, "Mate, you've been fucked."

Minsipi and Kepa moved away from the body of troops under the cover of the zooming bullets.

"Fire the signal pattern, again," Minsipi ordered his teen uncle as he energetically unveiled an ammo-box of bullets for his jungle relatives, "One shotgun round and two M16 shots."

As they waited for a response from the jungle men, they heard another death-scream from the soldiers they had come with.

Seconds later two dreadlocked men came running towards them while the rest kept pushing the government soldiers towards the Loruru. Minsipi admired them as they fought their way through the tangled growth. If only you were not my partners, you would be my catches of the day, he thought to himself and laughed.

"Hey, you fuckers!" Minsipi's near exhausted cousin shouted. "So, it's you that my dog spotted."

"Yes," Kepa said laughing. "Where is it and I'll kick it's arse?"

"No way," another rebel cried happily, "that's our body guard."

The rebels ceased fire and joined the meeting. The government forces were still occupied with rage and carelessly attacking the bush.

Regularly they had to duck onto the ground to avoid the straying bullets from the Loruru.

"Brothers, you know we were looking out for you," Ivini, the BRA commander said, nursing a captured rifle in his hand. "But as we were shooting one of them lost his senses and darted towards us; I fired at him and he dumped this rifle and disappeared, again."

"We need to disengage for the good of you brothers," Ivini directed. "We'll fire shots over your heads and you can run towards the Loruru."

"That's it," Kepa agreed, "otherwise, Nukuitu will suspect me and Minsipi."

"Whether peace dawns or not, that's the man I want to kill," Ivini hissed like a serpent. "Okay, go men!"

The two sprinted like thieves. Overhead bullets smashed into trees and wild bananas. Both fired into the air as they ran for the safety of the Loruru.

They crashed into the Loruru, speechless and exhausted; dragging with them, shrubs and creepers.

'Boys, there are hundreds of them!' Kepa shouted at the soldiers men. 'They are coming this way!"

The soldiers looked like the living dead. The great Resistant Commander, Nukuitu laid cold on the river bank.

"Just answer confidently at the junction of Heaven and Hell," Minsipi told Nukuitu's dead body over the buzzing flies and hungry ants.

The place was now quiet. Only a few cicadas shrilled in the bush as Fatnose sat in pain wondering about the things that had unfolded before his eyes.

"See you sometimes," a rebel shouted from a hillock above them. The soldiers responded with fire and swear words.

"Are we fighting humans or ghost?" the wounded Fatnose murmured in pain. "Let's go, men."

The company laid four dead resistant fighters and a soldier on stretchers and carefully tracked the Loruru's sandy banks to the road further downstream.

"Sorry, there are no more stretchers so please, do bear with us and walk for the good of our nation," Minsipi advised the wounded, feigning sadness.

Defeated and hopeless, Fatnose and his men - the good and the bad - staggered along through the thick undergrowth along the river bank.

Back in the camp, Minsipi sat quietly looking towards the Deuro Ranges and felt sad. Far inland, shouts of jubilations and gun shots were audible. They were answering the mortar explosions and concussion that now rumbled the hideouts.

"This is my country, Bougainville, bomb her but you shall never get to her heart," he said to himself and wiped tears from his eyes.

Ivitu - a redskin (Papua New Guinean) in the Buin language.

The title, Kamari nanka, means 'cold people' and also means 'coward' in the Kieta language.

11
WHEN JESUS STRIKES

"Teo'ri. Ningka'mau, wake up or I'll pour a bucket of cold water over you. It's time to pray," the boys' papa called.

"Teo'ri, do you hear me?" His tone was quite harsh. They sprang out of their bed because at any moment their fantastic papa would rush in like a gust of merciless wind and drag them out by their auricles.

The boys quietly galloped through the open door and sat cross-legged on the bare dusty floor

Their mama, Mimio, eyed them thoughtfully; as their little sister, Ame'a giggled, maybe for the joy of being cuddled. "Ningka'mau, you always sleep late, like a pregnant woman. You, two must start reacting swiftly; when it is prayer time, you know its prayer time," Mimio advised. "Do you hear me?" No one answered as they were lectured, not to be mean - but let the talker, talk.

"We'll start attaching you to a tether," Doka their papa, said soberly. With that he became the sign of the cross, "In the name of the father and of the son and of the Holy Spirit, Amen. I believe in God the father Almighty....."And it went on and on daily, as Teo'ri could remember.

In the heat of the afternoon sun, setting over Bai'aruai village in the western edge of Arawa, Teo'ri walked lazily through the Arawa High School main gate. It was three o'clock and he was homeward bound. He was a lone figure - like an adult shepherd - ahead of a troop of uniformed students.

Looking back, he admired the scene: students - all in yellow shirts and blue shorts scattered everywhere, against the background of pure greenness of the lawn and the swaying trees, notably mangoes, oranges and others that he could not name, looked so beautiful.

"Hey Teo'ri, *te nengtario!*" his friend Asina shouted from the fence adjacent to the main road. He did not bother to look back since the mass of students was fast gaining on him. But he slowed his pace and ambled leaving the footpath for the old bus stop shelter. He would wait there for his best buddy from his school days.

"Hey Asina, was calling for you," a passing girl called after him and for the some reason giggled with her companion.

"I heard him," Teo'ri answered her timorously without even looking at her direction.

"Hey Asina, why are you shouting my name among the students?" Teo'ri asked with a degree of annoyance at his buddy.

"For you to wait, you always go home early, as if you've got a child to care for. Or, do you?" They laughed gaily and started walking on.

"You know, Asina," Teo'ri speculated, "sometimes, I leave early since I get shagged too quickly meandering around."

"I see, we often get into the same boat, boy."

The two young men prowled, talking and laughing. A dozen metres at their side, the once life-saving Arawa General Hospital rested in ruins. So dull and brown, telling the world how insane was the Bougainvillean arsonist who had burnt this building down.

In front of them the Town House flats looked fine with its occupants sitting idly under the shade of their respective porches chewing betel-nut and smoking tobacco. Was this a special day? Someone new might wonder, because the whole street from the town houses to the Tupukaa'si Bridge was a single mass of students.

A lone truck dragging with it the stench of burning diesel quickly partitioned the yellow and blue mass. But as it passed by the student body came back as before, nicely. Asina and Teo'ri admired the manoeuvres ahead of them but talked about other issues.

They passed the Tupukaa'si Bridge and entered the town centre. From north came the rushing sound of waves on the beach. The air was sultry here.

Ahead the white house stood idle. The elephant grass surrounding it and its sister buildings swaying to the rhythm of the wind. The bamboo corner. A few shoppers and wanderers, and a couple of stray dogs, visited them, mostly to be ebbed of their contagious loneliness.

"Let's go eye shopping in Kung'kas," Asina suggested and headed for the entrance. Many eyes watched them approach, among them a cackle of giggling girls but they took no notice of those people and their follies and entered as if they were on an urgent shopping spree.

Inside, Teo'ri, was lost for words! A large portable stereo was displayed for any willing customer at seven hundred kina. It was alive with the hit lyrics of a certain Buka artist. The loud and clear woofing sound it gave touched him deep.

His ecstasy was not precipitous because the component, now in front of him already had a place in an exercise book that he kept. The newspaper cutting was glued there because Teo'ri admired and longed to own it. He had even thought of asking his uncle to purchase one for him but was ashamed to be seen as a beggar running after alms. So he had the picture kept and regularly, while in bed, or in the classroom, he would look at it and just admire it. Just love the picture till it hurts Teo'ri often thought.

Asina saw his friend transfixed. "*Aung*, you're acting as if you've never seen one before," he commented moving in his direction. "Looks good; but as fragile as glassware, you know, buy it today, and it malfunctions tomorrow." He tapped him on the shoulder.

Though Asina's remarks were not meant to harm, they really pierced his friend's heart and mind. He felt like sobbing but many eyes controlled him. To hold back the tears, he blinked automatically.

In a flashback to his early days; the days before his papa was gunned to his death, came to life; that life of living in accordance with the dictates of the Bible. "Own nothing of value as there are many brothers and sisters of ours, striving under the lacerating blade of poverty in Africa, America and many other places," his papa kept preaching. "Fight for the riches awaiting us in Heaven."

All this preaching, Teo'ri thinks, often with tears, now holds him and his siblings in an acute struggle through a quagmire of religion-oriented poverty. An irresponsible papa's life of fanaticism to religion created this mess for him in the other world, the world of secularism.

To Teo'ri the impact was dire: three years of high school without a pair of shoes; don't know how to drive, even though his father was a trained auto mechanic; no permanent home, even though his father was a long term employee of Bougainville Copper Limited; no sign of investment by his father and so on. He just left for his heaven without leaving anything for his children to depend on.

All this affected him. And his new awareness, apparent ever since he had entered school, provoked him further to denounce the Bible as a mere Jewish history used for turning the Melanesians insane enough to totally neglect the traditions that had shaped them for ages before the dawn of the damn European imperialism. In due course, his widowed mama had begun regularly bothering him about his careless attitude and remarks about religion. He had ceased attending church services some years back.

Both young men had their lower arms resting on the glass counter; that divided the shop. Half of it was where goods were displayed and the other section was left for the customers. Over cold drinks Asina had bought they listened to the music.

For a few moments, Teo'ri enjoyed the relieving impact of the cold drink and the music, but then was occupied by the fury of his misfortunes in life.

"You were right, *barau*," he said quietly to Asina. "To say I have never seen one of these." He sounded serious and upset.

"You told me once; your pa was a BCL employee - an auto mechanic. That Panguna mine, you know, had that money. Your late papa should have invested for you to reap the benefits today, you know," Asina said.

"Yes, but somewhere along the line, he met Jesus," Teo'ri retorted with a sigh "And that's that: No to investment for the children when he dies," he said. "Papa simply said that."

They walked out of the store and disposed of their empty cans into a bin and surprised an aging stray mongrel that leaped off, dragging behind a troop of pestering flies who regarded him as their lifelong partner.

"He was really an irresponsible man, your papa," Asina said soothingly. "To put you in such a sordid situation. Besides Jesus, wasn't he, some sort of a sot?"

"Not a drinker, *barau*."

"You see my papa every day, he has no trade like your papa but he worked tirelessly to make ends meet for us, his children," Asina sat on the lawn in front of the empty Arawa market. "Even before the crisis he bought a stereo and video set and so on to keep us from wandering about. On our only cocoa plot he also had a permanent house built."

Teo'ri felt defeated and cheated by his late papa and his living mama who, as he observed, was a victim of the burden forwarded from the ignorant past to the present. For his mother, without kind relatives, and because of her deep faith, poverty was unavoidable. He often drew the conclusion that if they had lived a balanced life in the past, today life would be more enjoyable and with meaning.

He came out of his deep thought, "You know I often admire you when you: drive vehicles, play guitars and keyboards and the like but for me - soon to reach thirty years of age – I know nothing of all these. Your papa was a responsible parent. He was telling me that he bought you all those things so that life was meaningful to you."

"Yes, he did exactly that and I really feel proud of papa, surely."

I have nothing to be proud of in regard to my papa, damn, Teo'ri told himself.

Sensing the air turning chilly and the piercing sound of the night time insects creeping in like a gush they left and went their separate ways with the whole contents of their talk clouded in their minds.

No one were to be seen on their respective streets; but the kitchen smoke creeping through the trees indicated that everyone was busy partaking in the preparation of the afternoon meal - fathers, mothers and children.

Teo'ri marched – in a lone bind - in deep thought, condemning his life as being useless and worthless. "I need to die early," he told himself, "Better to die and forget education and all that because my parents equipped me with absolutely nothing to face the new currents of secularism."

That night he laid in bed, wrapped up in a cloud of confusion, letting tears of self-pity run freely.

Te nengtario - just wait for me where you are.
Aung! – hey!

12
AKORE AND HER SONS-IN-LAW

As I left my beloved island, it was engulfed in a long armed political struggle for survival. Thousands lost their lives, fighting each other; a few were just slaughtered for no good reason by the fighting factions. This was self-grown anarchy going on behind the Papua New Guinean and Australian manned blockade on the poor island.

Despite all this and the tears that I continuously shed for my people, I successfully obtained a BA degree in Social Work from the University of Papua New Guinea and married a fine Bougainvillean woman from the Wakunai District on the northern edge of Central Bougainville.

And as the fragile - but carefully managed - peace process slowly gained momentum, I resigned from my former job in PNG and returned back to my roots - this is where I am now - to serve my own people.

Also, I came home to live a harmonious life among the family that I had missed for at least a decade. A family - to me - that must be responsible, hardworking and co-operatively striving for the general betterment of the extended family. On the whole, I personally, as a young man, then, felt that working hand-in-hand as a family in these economically desperate times was a need for all the societies of Bougainville.

But for my extended family this wasn't so. My family, that had kept to our roots in Pomaua village, were absolutely parasitic in their dealings with me. All they wanted was free handouts from me. Free money for school fees, clothes and you name it.

On the other hand, my elder sister, Ketunani, who my mama had chased out of Pomaua when her children were not yet born, lived a life I openly admired and accepted. Her children were doing fine in the high schools and universities. So, naturally, I was more tilted to my sister Ketunani, than to Mama and her favourite daughters, Taruito and Mime'raa.

She was a very independent woman with her husband. I admired her industriousness very much. For, even though, her two daughters, Botuto and Ipiona, resided with me and attended school, she did not expect me to feed them. She hated being a liability of some sort to me, I think.

One halcyon day, as my mama and her daughters left after scolding me and my wife, I sat under my house exploring the profundities of my Pomaua family's disrespectful attitude towards me and my wife.

Women own land here in this matrilineal society; they have power over the land, but what was wrong? Was it my hussy mama's influence? Or my brother-in-laws? The Bougainville crisis? I was lost, since the only obvious answer under the sun was irresponsibility. Laziness and ignorance was gobbling these people inside-out!

I was at the peak of this notion when my nieces walked in through the gate. "Uncle, what's bothering you?" they chorused melodically. They were clever, I thought, to read my mind.

"These idiots ...." I began but was interrupted.

They sang in interest: "Who?"

"Your grandma and her daughters in Pomaua," I paused to search for words. "They came here for money, today."

Seeing that my nieces were paying attention to my words, I continued: "Grandma came for five hundred kina to buy a live pig - a gift - for her namesake; whilst, Taruito asked for some money for her children's school fees. When I said that I had no money, they fired up at me and went off."

The eldest of my two nieces was sympathetic with me

and my wife. "Bastards, they say they own all the land in Pomaua; and where is the profit from it? Do they think you are a merchant bank or something! Cheap liars!" she was frantic.

"The problem, my nieces, is that they don't see that I have a family to care for," I said pleadingly, "when our nation is struggling through the sharp blades of soaring inflation it is hard. And even when the cost of living is so high they still think we've got money that's not needed in the future."

A utility, making horribly loud grunts with its unmaintained exhaust-pipe entered our street. I thought it would not reach the u-turn in front of my residence, but it came. On the tray two elderly men were talking and laughing over intoxicating betel-nut. They came and parked beside my neighbour's premises and were welcomed by the angry dog there. There they remained without killing the engine.

My wife was cooking upstairs and Botuto went to help her, leaving me and Ipiona, downstairs.

Above our heads, in the house, my wife, Daisy, was moving everywhere engaged to chores known only to her.

I quietly monitored her pacing down the corridor and into the restroom. There, the septic was flushed. Then on the veranda she was. "Two, can you please come up," her voice was sweetly calm, "come and eat this while we wait for the chef, Botuto to finish."

On the table, hors d'oeuvres were prepared. I just could not wait and started gobbling like a hungry child.

"My lass, where did you get this from?" I asked, demandingly as if I was an inspecting the gourmet food.

My wife stared at me with surprise but then chuckled and said: "Your termagant mama gave it to me."

With her auburn hair she looked beautiful and the thought of kissing her caught me but I reluctantly saved it for the bed.

"Sometimes she is a good woman," I said over a

mouthful of salad. "Anyway, you two have to tell me more about those fathers of yours." The girls glimmered with laughter over that suggestion.

I wanted to know more about my brother-in-laws since I was away when my sisters got married. What was their attitude to life? Are they the sort good-at-the-art-of-producing-a-child for me to look after but staying away just because I'm a government worker.

My job denied me time at home with family. The little breaks that I had were mostly was dedicated to my wife who, by tradition, had no rights in Kieta society - only in her own culture in Wakunai. So in the pleasure of the relishing dishes I waited for an interesting discourse - whether it was biased or not I didn't care. I displayed a burning credulity in my complexion.

To start my hesitant nieces off, I began: "From my observations, I see Oriui as the laziest creature on earth, what do you think, Ipiona?" I prompted, referring to my sister Taruito's husband.

"Aung kongto, masika si-darori kaka'ruaa," Ipiona said, as Daisy excused herself and headed into the kitchen. 'That house they now live in is now deteriorating at an alarming rate. It was built by Oriui's papa, so many years ago.'

Hearing the rusty and noisy car at our neighbours taking off she paused, craning her neck to see them off.

"Even now," Botuto said joining the conservation, her left palm hesitantly chafing a tablespoon, "as the house is falling apart, it doesn't bother him. You know, when it rains with wind they usually end up in grand mama's."

"Isn't that funny," Daisy joined in from the kitchen sink, *"mi save lukim tambu blong yu bilas gut na raun lo taim ol liklik blong yu raun wantaim brukbruk kolos stap lo peles. Yu mas sindaunim ol pastaim."*

"Exactly," Ipiona backed her aunty with a shrug, "you need to see them. I was not prepared to shoulder the burden of shame when my cousins began stealing clothes from others because their fathers are there sleeping."

As an afterthought, Botuto added, "And you know what, they arranged for Mimera to marry Tarupiu because she was then not living in proper housing. They said he was a good builder of fine houses, so they persuaded Akore to allow her to marry him. But all he builds today are those makeshift shelters."

Everyone broke into laughter, when Daisy stated, "If you tell Tarupiu to build a house, he would solemnly say, "*Ol driman yu wokim lo gutpla haus; bai mi stil wokim lo rabis haus stap.*"

"That would exactly be that stupid's talk," Botuto remarked hopelessly and doddered off to her room.

"Last weekend when we went there," I said to Daisy and Ipiona, "I felt pity for my little nephews. They scolded each other over a few cocoa trees planted by mama. You know that talkative son of Mimera, Tobonu had more cocoa pods than the others and a row erupted. Tobonu swore badly at his cousins.

"When I intervened, Tobonu darted into the bushes in fear. Sad, you know, but I just told them, later when peace resumes they must tell their parents to plant more cocoa trees and they just laughed to my wonder."

Daisy smirked. "It's your obligation, Masibai, to try and make them see what's bad about them."

"Yes, you need to sit and talk to them," Ipiona, who was enjoying the feeling of Daisy's palms on her hair, interrupted. "Make them see that you are not responsible for what their husbands should be doing."

"Anyway, I'll try," I said. "But, I know the Kieta saying - you can only straighten up a tree when it is still young and growing."

I wondered all night in my bed. Daisy's snores did not bother me. "I'll make it for the weekend," I told myself. "I'll set them up and try injecting morality into those big heads." Then I slipped off into that silvery world of my dreams.

The Saturday sun, so bright in the azure sky, caught me

wandering about, around the empty village of Pomaua. Nobody was around; all had gone off to their gardens early and all around as far as the eyes could see, garden fires coloured the whole Apiatei range blue. All the people were out but not my family members, who were still sleeping.

Beyond the edge of the village; and downstream along the Araba brook, where my family owns the land, no one was there with those few unkempt cocoa trees. I was annoyed, for just adjacent to me and on the other side of the Araba, the cocoa trees had their minders around them. This area was used by the landless clans in this great village of ours.

Married to the traditionally rich clan's women, my brother-in-laws were not there toiling the land, but were elsewhere, minding their farts.

The swaying of the cocoa trees made me sad, as they were the last, excluding the coconut palms, evidence of my late papa's labouring hands. The memory of my hardworking papa landed on me just like the sharp claws of a cat on a mouse as I passed his grave going towards Mimera's home.

"Eh, Tobonu," I surprised my peeing nephew, "you are so late, where are the rest?" I laughed as he nearly clamped his penis zipping up but he grinned at the lucky miss.

"All are sleeping," his young voice answered. "Only Mimera went looking for firewood to cook the food that grandmamma will bring from her garden later." For a few minutes his gaze thoroughly scanned me, then he asked, "When did you come?"

"Yesterday night. When they come, tell them, uncle said we will have some talk in the afternoon at Akore's." I left him looking quite lost.

As the sun slowly liberated itself from the grip of Pokpok island in the distant east on her journey home and came overhead the shadows that I and the other things cast on the ground became shorter. The air was also turning humid and unbearable. I was perspiring profusely as were the chickens next to me, though we were all under the shade of the orange tree outside Mama's house.

Mama, a well-known early bird in the family, arrived with a load of taro. Later she would be distributing that to all the households of her daughters, thus denying the independence of their marriages.

"Hey, son," she enquired, as she dropped the sack on the ground next to me, "what sort of talk are we having? Tobonu just told me down the road." She looked at me with seriousness and then, added, "Son, did you bring me some money?"

"*Moni, otoa, e-ani,*" I chuckled to the fury that didn't hide on her complexion.

"*Oi, baka,*" She sat beside me, "what do you work for son? Don't hide if you work for tobacco sticks like your forefathers in the German days." She laughed rudely, picking up a bag of kaukau and ambling to the tap in the centre of the Akore's lawn. Then, as an afterthought, she added, mockingly, "E, I know, that Wakunai bags it all.."

I was infuriated. My chest was trembling; but she wasn't a male to receive my fist on that wrinkled face of hers. And over the rim my anger spilled verbally, "Why are you saying all this senseless talk, idiot?" I demanded. My voice was strident. A couple of my nephews rushed to witness the paroxysm. "You are the most contumacious lady in all Pomaua, ma'am."

She, with her weak hearing, couldn't decode my 'contumely' in meaning or words. "What are you saying?"

"What, what," I snarled. "You mother of self-imposed paupers."

Tears ran down her cheeks like torrential rain. "I never knew...," she sobbed, "that you are this kind of a son with such ugly parlance. Also, I am not a pariah or a mendicant as you say." She shot a kaukau through the window sending broken louvers to the ground. "Do you feed me always? I work this land while you feign being a white man in Arawa."

Pity ran through my veins for my mama, but I decided to attack her devotion to feeding my married sisters. "Mama, your words are true, but you labour your little strength away and work for these lazy in-laws of yours and their children when they should be caring for you."

"What you saying," She screamed, after misinterpreting me point, "aren't they my children?"

"Yes, they are your children," I shouted back, my voice, again was tense. "Those lazy bastards. They never help you in your gardens, but still you feed them and to complement you they produce more children, isn't that so?"

Then, I picked up my haversack and marched towards the purling Araba. I was set for Arawa and never to be back in this senseless place.

"Go away...go away," Mama exclaimed in between her sobs. "Never come back, you man with no tradition and without respect for your in-laws."

I dipped my legs into the coldness of the water; enjoying the refreshing sensation, I called back, "They are your husbands, women."

"*Orara da! Orara da! Mosika*," She began throwing her sweet potatoes at me.

I looked back and saw Taruito consoling her. "Never set your foot here, again," she cried with determination. "Go die in Wakunai ... you only favour Ketunani's children."

Though, Mama did lose sight of me her shouts and curses and condemnations still echoed through the stillness of the bush.

Oh my God, the place I was united to by ties of consanguinity, stubbornness was kicking me out of so hard.

Defeated, I rambled for Arawa through the perpetual calmness of the forest cover and the music of the birds and insects.

Paa-pa – uncle.

Aung kongto, masika si-darori kaka'ruaa - really, your brother-in-law is a lazy man.

Mi save lukim tambu blong yu bilas gut na raun lo taim ol liklik blong yu raun wantaim brukbruk kolos stap lo peles. Yu mas sindaunim ol pastaim - I see your brother-in-law dressing so neat whilst his children live in rags.

Ol driman yu wokim lo gutpla haus; bai mi stil wokim lo rabis haus stap - dreams you have in a good house is also, what I have.

Moni, otoa, e-ani - no money, my dear.

Oi, baka! – oh please!

Oi, baka orara da! orara da! mosika – oh you bad! You bad! Dog like!

13
BANTOKA PLACE

"So…so, here you are come back," old Dentana is happily welcoming his grandson. "So quick you made it Maate. I last saw you at the market; or maybe at the junction of Kereitu Street. I am not sure with my memory because of my age. Was it where your uncle lives a few streets up at Section 15, Asita Street, just in the vicinity of your school, Tupukas Primary."

Maate sits in the room admiring the family photographs, framed and neatly hanging, scattered across the wall. So many there are; Grandpa smiling in his teens; Grandpa and Grandma in Honiara; Grandpa and Maate at the abandoned Panguna mine in the 1980s and on and on the list goes.

Standing against the wall opposite the window is the festooned Madonna. "This is a real sanctum," Maate is whispering to himself. "Why am I here Grandpa?"

Nobody knows that though. Grandpa has every photograph he owns in the room that Maate is occupying while he is attending school. Grandpa has also chosen the school for him to attend - the very school that his aunties attended so many years ago.

The reasons are Grandpa's alone but deep down Maate knows why his grandfather favours him so much. It is because his looks are those of his grandma. This is why Grandpa takes him for his blue-eyed boy. He loves him the most and often prays for him with his rosary for his success in life.

Without a door is Maate's room, only Grandpa's has one. Passing from the entrance, he goes to the end of the wall that separates his room from the dual purpose lounge and dining room adjoining the tiny kitchen. He had been exploring to see what the old man is doing; stirring up chinking sounds and talking to himself.

"Kaaka, what you doing?" he asks, after a brief moment of hesitation.

"Preparing a little chowder just for you, kaaka," the feeble voice in the kitchen is calling back. "Would you mind running up to Section 16 Tonguru Street - there's a canteen there - and get a packet of rice? The money is there on the table behind you." Dentana is pointing at a table that occupies almost 30 percent of the lounge-dining room.

Maate carefully makes his way through the dirty puddle-infested Bantoka Street. He knows that many years ago this street was wide enough for two cars to run side by side. Today, creeping thorny grass, called *dongasi* in the Kieta language, and other creepers and plants have squeezed it to a mere one and half metres wide.

"Hi, Maate, you are at school here now?" disabled Tonama, is asking while busying his lips with his mouth organ and somehow talking at the same time.

With just a nod of his head, Maate ambles on.

The giant Pikus tree captures his attention, so he slows down as a car speeds up the Rumba Road. Its tyres screech loudly as it passes Doraka Street ahead.

"Stop admiring that damn tree," Jackie says, approaching him.

She is a teenager and, unlike him, a Basikanung of the Kurabaang clan. One of the clans his traditions permits him to marry into. Furthermore, her accent suggests that she is from the Panguna area. She is one of the Ioroan love singers of the rugged mountains.

"Just admiring the view," Maate is frankly saying.

"That's a waste of time; acting like a tourist. Soon you will be admiring the view of me," Jackie says with a mocking laugh and saunters on slowly. Then she adds:

"Right in my room."

"Thank you. And, when?"

"When time permits, my boy," Jackie says. They venture on their separate ways in suspense.

A swollen shopping bag dangling in hand, Maate is standing outside the screen door rubbing dirt from the soles of his shoes on the worn flood mat. From the kitchen, and permeating through the air, is the delicious smell of food that is making him hungry. So he enters with high hopes of tasting Grandpa's stew.

"Oh Maate, the stew is being cooked," Grandpa says as he licks a spoon like a child. "Now, it's your turn to boil the rice."

The sun is setting over the western ridges as the afternoon breezes set in with steaming calmness and the pair is comfortably sitting around the dinner table, spoons chinking and tingling on the fragile glass bowls.

The meal is perfect to the oldie, who considers himself, the best cook around Kieta. "Maate, is this stew made by an old bone okay?" he asks joyfully.

"Very nice," Maate is saying, decanting the final remains of his bowl into his wide mouth. He is a glutton.

"Tha...n...k you," the oldie, says with a sort of grogginess to Maate's surprise.

"Kaaka, what is it?" says the grandson, fearfully.

"Not...hing," the old man twitches, sweeping his plate to the floor. Then, the wriggling body lands with a bang next to it. For minutes, he struggles there as the grandson stands like a guard affixed by fright. His mouth is wide open and saliva is trickling down his fat lips.

Recollecting his senses: "Finis?" Maate is staring at the grizzled head; then he bends to check if there is still a pulse. Alive, he discovers. His heart is beating loudly.

Maate wets him with a moist tea-towel and he comes to his senses. He assists him to a chair.

"You know, my child," the sick fella sobs in self-pity,

"I've completed me gradation in life; and this life is at the brim ready to go. That's why I suffer a lot with ailments like trances and many others." He pauses in thought. Then adds, "But this house is what I don't want to lose ...." Something distracts him. He is thinking?

"Don't want to lose, why?" the youngster is prompting to squeeze out the reasons.

"This old house, Maate, is where my life was moulded. From here I got your grandma, whose death denied her the joy of growing old together with me. Your mother and uncles and aunts were born here. Here is where, our spirits belong." His eyes water but he continues. "Because of my intense love for this domicile - after the Bougainville crisis - I reclaimed it for you; for in you, your grandma dwells, so there is light at the end of the tunnel in you. He looks around the room, then adds in finality, "In case, if you need to know, this house is on Section 14. The house, on the maps of Arawa, is numbered 143 and it is located on Bantoka Street. If you sell it, you will disadvantage yourself."

Maate is lost for words seeing this very intimate bond between the old man and the house. He is thinking how his grandpa left home and migrated into town after the war. "So, Grandpa is only going back home in his coffin," he is telling himself. Back at home, in Paraiano, his kinsmen are calling him and are waiting for him and his coffin.

Night time cicadas and other insects are shrilling outside. Added to the disturbances is the howling of dogs in their mating and the wind was blowing the branches of the mighty Pikus tree to and fro sending ripe seeds onto the rooftops with unpleasant thudding sounds. Thud upon thud until Maate begins his session of profound snoring in resistance.

A remarkable fortnight is just whistling by. A memorable fourteen days; one of them - a pleasant

Tuesday - witnessed Maate losing his dogged virginity to the *kurabanang*, Jackie, of house number 171 in Doraka Street. So swiftly the days are fading, just like the shooting stars in the night sky.

Since his arrival in town, Maate knows that his grandpa's life is hanging on a thread - ready to go. The fact that he lives in this beloved little red house is jam-packed with the disturbing trepidation of finding himself sleeping under a single roof with a dead man. This goads him into regularly overnighting across the road in Asita Place. In the mornings he lies to the old fella, saying that he took refuge from molesting drunks and other reasons that are too many and are absorbed by the old man grain by grain.

But on this fateful night, muffled up in a thick blanket, is Maate, struggling against the cold in this strange morose darkness. He is feeling spirits from distant places hovering around his grandpapa in an angelic dance. Fuggy is the air. Sweat begins to trickle down his body so he unwraps and gropes his way outside to be welcomed by two fireflies orbiting merrily around the veranda post. He knows that fireflies are the agents of death.

"Kaaka, is it you and Tete?" he asks the fireflies as he passes to a seat on the moist lawn.

In the open, he feels safe from the spirits' daring plucks. But his belief in fireflies as the actual physical form of death is confusing him. He is now watching their airborne strutting, like a boy transfixed by a nymphet, as they are disappearing behind the house. And to his surprise, they are dancing around him again; bumping into his side restlessly. Other straying mates are also teaming up for this ritualistic masquerade. Then, seemingly bored they are now withdrawing, leaving behind a lone fly that orbits around Maate twice and then departs as the first cock crow in the neighbourhood begins before dawn.

The sun is high as the morning breeze peacefully blows sleep out of the abodes of Arawa. The sky is cerulean, like the sea and Maate is lying embraced in sleep beside the flower bed. A neighbour sees him and wakes him up. "Hey, Maate why are you asleep here?" he asks.

"I just wanted to," he lies as he rubs off dirt from his side and dashes into the house to wake the old fella.

He goes to his grandpa's door to confirm his nightmare. His left palm firmly grips the door knob, turns it to set the door ajar and hesitantly peeps in. He carefully looks at the resting figure. The old man's chest is not moving up and down with the intake of fresh air and the unleashing of waste air out. "Kaaka, are you still sleeping?" he asks, but no answer comes. Instead, an ant creeps out of the old man's nostril; he is dead. Peacefully dead in the house that he loved the most.

Maate is rushing out of the room. "Kaaka, why did you do this to me?" he is wailing. "Why did you desert me?" He is rolling and singing a mourning song on the gravel and dirt of the lawn and sympathetic neighbours are rushing in to comfort him.

Early the next morning, Maate sits in the open back of a Land Cruiser in a convoy of cars bringing home his grandpa's casket. A red Hilux is carrying the casket in front as the others follow behind. Slowly, they climb up Ako Hill on the eastern-most fringe of Arawa in suffocating diesel fumes.

"Kaaka, you loved the little red house numbered 143 on Bantoka Street," Maate is saying to himself. "I will, however, love the little green house numbered 171, where Jackie dwells in Doraka Street. That's where my spirit is locked."

The convoy is hidden by the bend at Karukate; Arawa is gone from Maate's sight and slowly, they descend down Keuru brae and onto the coconut palm-covered Kereinari plains

Kaaka - grandfather/grandson in Nasioi language.
Tete – grandmother.

14
I AM GOING BACK TO MY ROOTS

Bali Bris, Kimbe. It is here, by the soothing sounds and smell of the sleepy Bismarck Sea I am beseeching my soul to tell me where is my Bougainville? Where am I heading to after all the years in the Solomon Sea? Here I am, I have taken a step with a stinging pain in my heart go across this unpredictable sea in the cover of the falling night.

I am going to Bali, the birth place of my father. I am going to see my broken hearted-grandmother, who has being wishing and weeping to see me before she follows her dear son to the tomb. But I am going empty handed and not with the remains of my father who I have killed on Bougainville. But I am going, after years of weeping silently to see and set my feet on that mystery in the Bismarck Sea I am going with a broken heart.

My *toto* keeps telling me the tales of this mystery sea and our island, Bali, somewhere in the midst of the expanse of sea before my eyes. She talks about the beauty of the night before us from this dancing trawler; the shoal of flying fish and the drifting logs on the way to the Witu Islands makes a voyage memorable. She is singing.

"Have you ever crossed the sea, *toto*?" Toto enquires.

With my eyes on the silhouetted Kimbe Island, I can only nod, "Never, never and never," accompanied by a distant chuckle.

"Poor you, *toto*," Toto laughs.

The wheel-man of our trawler, *MV Kathleen,* passes before us with a mouthful of areca nut and gives a distant thumbs-up to his crewmen, who just shine so bright in the smile of the sea. They are the sea because they love the sea that I fear. I fear it because Panguna in Bougainville has no sea for me to love.

Then came a casket; they said he was a relative of mine who had died in Port Moresby. He was a chief of a place they said was Penata on Bali Island where I belong. He was so beautified with flowers and clean clothing, wrapped to sleep for the night long journey.

My *toto* ushers me forward to the tiny ship. I am lost. I think about the giant waves that sea people talk about. I fear that a sea raging upon us would be worse if we have a casket on board. But I had no hope; I had to go across this sea of mystery that my papa's people love so much.

My *toto* shakes my hands and wishes me a safe trip home to Bali.

I make my way to the back and secure a position on a petrol drum. From this spot I can see and admire the foamy water that is stirred up by the drive propellers beneath the hull.

From here I also get a good view of the few people I am with for this voyage. There are three mothers with tear stained eyes; there is a cackle of colleens who keep smoking and chewing betel nut and there is a trio of ship staff men who march about like hovering house flies.

The little *Kathleen* throttles and quakes. The smell of diesel fumes blanket us as one of the people on the wharf, whose feet above us I can see, removes the mooring line and hands it over to the crew who greedily hide it where it belongs.

The ship is going down the river, cutting through drifting debris, tin cans that humans have littered in Kimbe Town. I watch the town fading. The huge oil palm tanks that stand too proud on the skyline of Kimbe Town grow smaller every second and I feel like crying for leaving the land for the mercy of this great river. But I am okay, for I have left Bougainville to set my foot on that special island in the midst of the Bismarck Sea.

A boy comes to me. "Brother, don't you worry. The villagers will cry over you for you are bringing your late father back to his island of birth.". He makes me shed a tear.

I lower my head and fight back tears. My eyes fixed on the palm infested Talasia coast to the west, which our *Kathleen* is navigating parallel to for Bulu Point up north. I wondered if there is a god was there on Mount Hela to redeem me from this pain. I look upon Mount Bere, but it is snoring. I skim my eyes up Mount Habuna looking for a god of peace, but there are none there because Bougainville is a stranger to them.

A shoal of flying fish disturbs me. I look into the water as they submerge into the eternity of the sea. Then I look back at Kimbe but she is now a dot for we have made distance past Garua Plantation at Talasia Station. I am travelling fast into the unknown mystery of the sea.

As the ship decreases the distance to Bali every hour, I am weeping more and more, deep in my heart. But I am going; going with a broken heart and empty hands for my withered New Guinean grandmother.

Mount Vakori, the tallest peak on the Talasia Peninsula, pities not a lost Bougainvillean tourist. It keeps on torturing me: Where are my kin? Where is my blood? Where is my son, you killer Bougainvillean? I had no strength for a fight so I let the tears run freely down my cheeks and hid in my jacket to sneeze.

Kathleen conquers the Talasia Peninsula past Bulu and rain falls with lightening. Night settles in and cold penetrates the marrow of my bones. I look out to sea, but there is no life except the flicker of lightening above us.

The boy, who my Kimbe *toto* has ordered to take care of me, is always there for me giving me strength and peace of mind with his stories and areca nut. We are a family of mourners around the coffin positioned between us.

A single light is put on to illuminate the deck and a Rastafarian mother cuddling her sleeping child looks at me hard. She calls the boy who had being orbiting around me for so long and asks, "Who is this stranger?"

After their short chat the world awakes. "People;

people, we have on board two chiefs of Penata," she weeps in a strange language speaking of my father's people. Pointing at my position she says: "There is Mataio, our living chief who has come across the sea from Bougainville and here is our dead chief of Penata." She slams the coffin with her hand and weeps hysterically and adds, "Toto; my *toto*, why have you come when I am mourning?"

I shed tears and give her my back. My minder also sheds tears as sorrow creeps into our midst. The rain eases and the sea is pacified by our broken hearts. And our vessel churns on proudly in the darkness that our eyes cannot penetrate.

Our trawler gallops on with confidence despite my doubts of arriving home in harmony with the mysterious sea.

By dawn my eyes become heavier with the stress of the long sleepless journey as I sit on the drum. But I fought away the bothering sleep to watch the sea and listen to the hisses upon a lost Bougainvillean tourist.

As the sun began to chase away the dark, islands appear and I am told that they are the Witu group. Our *Kathleen* braves its way far south of them as it heads straight for Bali, somewhere in this midst of a sea expansive beyond my expectations.

The people who had occupied the front of the wheel house saw it first and my guardian angel came close and lectures me. "Brother, those are the Kumburi sister mountains of your land." But I saw no mountains and wondered. But as the vessel steamed closer, it was true; really, they were mountains so steep.

My minder kept talking. "On the other side of these mountains are your homes Makiri, Manopo, Penata, Nigilani and the land of Vamangama. Our only running river is the Boroko that is sourced at the foot of the Kumburi Mountains. From Manopo you will come and we can play at the Nughutu islet and cove or we can paddle to our fishing and hunting island of Ragha to hunt for wild pigs and birds. It's fun there."

"Yes, *toto*," the Rastafarian *toto* hugs me and weeps, "This is your island. This is where I cared for you many years ago when you were a child with your late father and mother."

I cannot control the emotions in my heart and warm tears began profusely running down my cheeks. I was crying for coming empty-handed for my withering grandmother and my home of Bali Island.

Toto – aunty/nephew.

15
THE WRONG LOVE OF TONAU'A

Warning: Some readers may find some parts of this short story challenging and even offensive

The long winding Kokore ridge stretches west from Guava village on the Crown Prince Range. Calmly and patiently, the sun tracks her spine every day giving birth to the fecund rainforest that covers the fine rolling hills below. Wild rainbow waterfalls and happy children play along the Tonau'a tributary; the only known noisy brook in the valley of Tumpusiong, yonder west.

This is a perfect paradise, a sanctum for the carefree naked little kids and the morally cautious older children of the numerous scattered jungle hideouts of the runaway refugees from the bluish Mananau plain in the Nagovis district of South Bougainville.

The Tonau'a Brook was freedom from the attacking Papua New Guinean army that, with its mortars, had recently murdered dozens of innocent children in Buin. Also, it was democracy; but a democracy that the young Tobo'nu could not enjoy after being sexually abused by her devilish stepfather. It was a freedom cup full to the brim with sour honey for the poor teenage belle.

The singing birds could never succeed in liberating her emotionally dead soul; she was forever locked in a dark and grubby prison of guilt, shame and stress. Oh, did we fight for the betterment of Bougainvilleans or what?

Poor Tobo'nu's guilt, shame and stress came about by coincidence one night. Satan – the pot-bellied padre preaching excitedly in front of all the fresh garden produce of the land brought to him as offertory is a practical angel on Earth. A man of action and not a baseless theory proposer of ideas that have the day's politicians sick in the head and resorting to corruption because their dreams turn to be so fruitless for the people of the nation.

The father, Tonepa, came home late one October night during the rainy season in the Panguna area of the Republic of Bougainville from an arduous military operation in Mananau to the south-west, and discovered that his sexy new wife, formerly, a widow, was not home for his warm-up of another kind, the type that renews and refreshes the soul of a human being who had just arrived home after a near-death encounter with the invading New Guinean army, a sex dinner.

His wife's warm thighs and the promise of coitus were not there to welcome him home or placate his burning desire. His routine was shattered like the sudden fade of lightening in the night sky.

He sat on the porch warming himself over the flickering fire, eating freshly baked *ino* left for him by his wife, and called with frustration: 'Tobo'nu, where is your mama, Murubita?'

"Mama went for the funeral upstream at Pan'sinare. Can't you hear the funeral songs sweeping down our way with the scurrying, blustering and rollicking wind, Papa?" Her voice was sweet and calm, "The young and laughing girl, Nebunu, just died from lack of medicine."

"Oh, sexy, I can't hear. Maybe the M203 grenades the foe fired have deafened my ears," he lied with a chuckle. "Anyway, I am very sorry for her, but it's also good that some are going ahead so that they can plant rice for those of us that will follow later."

"Oh, you are so ruthless about your clanswoman," Tobo'nu sighed.

"Hmm, that's why we die, to go ahead and prepare the ground for the latecomers so that when they come, to their surprise, there is a naked girl for them." He bent and lit his pipe.

Deep in the core of his heart, he was burning with lust. Ethics were at war in the midst of his mind's impenetrable marshland: "Be careful!" the good side cried.

But, the bad side kept singing in his unstable emotional world:

> *"O woman of the Mananau plain*
> *Why deny me an erotic dance in this cold night.*
> *I your love, your freedom and justice…*
> *Why run away to the peak of adultery*
> *Where those men shall dirty you*
> *And make me sick…why?*
> *Here is your flower on my bed and under my roof;*
> *Not my fruit, but your fruit*
> *For I did not take your hymen, you*
> *Road flower of a distant bee.*
> *This is my love. The compliment of my strife*
> *To defend the land and you.*
> *The gains of war…price of sacrifice.*
> *This is my song.*
> *A beautiful and chaste mother*
> *Of*
> *Mananau Plains*
> *After you go with the floods."*

He stooped low with his eyes fixed to the fire and his mind on the bed and coercing Tobo'nu for love. He was whispering to her: "Hey, I am your love. Your mama is old for me. Let's make love, let's make love, pleaseeee."

Inside the dark makeshift hut with no doors, Tobo'nu ignored his joking which she was so familiar with. But that fickle heart was a mystery. She was an innocent bird in the trap of the adults' world. Since her real father was killed in Buka while fighting the PNG forces, she and her beloved mother had found themselves in the hands of this fierce-looking gunman.

He was a caring young man, however; never as yet exposed to marriage with another woman. But somehow he fell in love with a widow against the wishes of his parents, and that burning desire for any attractive woman was yet to be appeased. The sight of a girl often had his heart jumping high.

Ha-ha, some good love bites he had had from an experienced widow, but he just could not let this one go! His wife's little immaculate flower had had him sick with love for a while and that night was the worst. Now, at his reach she was, however!

"When is she coming back, girly girl?" he said, his heart beating faster, as he placed his gun on the bed he was sitting on.

"Tomorrow morning," she said, lazily from the dark. She was an invisible goddess!

"And why didn't you go?" he asked, feebly. "Oh! I didn't know you are on a date," he added, with a sarcastic laugh, as an afterthought.

"Ah! Who are you on a date with?" Tobo'nu insisted as she got her agile body into a prone position. Her breasts were flat against the mat and a thick blanket was over to fight off the intruding cold. "Stop your lies and go to sleep."

"Ah, stop speaking like a scarlet woman. Oh, where will I sleep, by the way?"

"Have you forgotten your bed?" she laughed, drowsily.

"Yes, I think so but I need some warm thighs right now."

"Run to Pan'sinare, then," Tobo'nu mumbled, with the heavy mass on her eyelids and her brain turning into the strange new world of her dreams.

Tonepa stood up and unsteadily entered with his gun and fumbled in their huge common bed for something that was non-existent. His heart was nearly bursting free from his chest and sweat was wrapping up his neck as Tobo'nu's body odour engulfed and aroused him like some malignant illness of his loins that must be addressed soon.

Outside the wind was cruel to the trees and fireflies.

His little hut, however, just laughed at the wind in pure mockery since it was too safe from the menacing tentacles.

He was droopy in his legs and feeling sexy so he lay in his space on the bed. The air he was breathing was sour to his mental lungs. He needed to crawl outside again and seek some fresh air. He went, touching the lightly snoring baby of his wife, who was off from reality on her teenage supple legs. The touch was cool to his soul.

Outside he relaxed in the cool mountain breeze rolling down from Pan'sinare as he monitored the surroundings for any infiltrative human activity that could disturb him. He hated tell tales or snoopers. Fireflies wandered like lost sheep around him. The *patu'ai* (funeral song) was clear but uninteresting to him.

He spat into the air and cautiously re-entered and onto the bed. Close to Tobo'nu, who was now resting on her right shoulder, he laid listening attentively to the rhythm of the snores; a midnight animal physician at work on a dead butterfly.

He moved closer and slid his hairy right hand like a snake beneath Tobo'nu's nape and had her head resting on his elbow; he was a loving father to a sick child, in the night hours. In the sun, by his wife, this would have been scary.

The lovely bird snored peacefully. She was resting calmly like the sea at night during low water with reefs so vulnerable.

Tonepa was quickly into the blanket, heart pounding heavily and got her. Into her Elysian world, he penetrated his way like an elver through a tiny opening that its rigid body was painfully making. She gave a determined struggle. But she lacked the power of resistance in the night where there was no mercy.

Her thin hands flew everywhere for support. Her fine legs lost strength with the weight they supported. Her scratching was not doing enough for her liberation, for deep down in her virgin veins, a flood of pleasure and pain crept to switch off her heart. She would be dead sooner or later and she was not ready for this skirmish.

She was drowning in a tempestuous sea, as she cried in agony from an unknown love: 'Who are you? Oh! Dog, who are you? Hiiii! Hi.' She was stupefied.

No word came from Tonepa. He had a virgin at his disposal - the daughter of his sexually skilled wife - so he worked hard for the long dreamt moment of climax. For far too long his wife had been laughing at his early orgasms when she had made love to him; and now, he was the one making love to his wife's daughter.

She gave one last cry of agony and succumbed:

"Who are you?
Oii! Oii. Iiii.
You Tonepa, my mother's husband?
O you dog...You
Liar and cheat.
Liar an..."

The sun came early the next day. Birds cried peacefully in the dancing canopies as Tobo'nu lay weak and unable to walk. Blood had the bed stained rosy and a urine smell diffused through the room every moment she attempted to move.

"Tobo'nu, Tobo'nu please where are you?" her mama called from the *kopero* outside. "You sleep well my love. Did your papa come?'

Not an answer came from a human being except from the little birds that criss-crossed the jungle. The little hideout was deathly silent and in grief. The voice that welcomed nature was somewhere else.

Calmly, Murubita, came to the porch with a bucket of water for cooking. Around the fireplace were military boot prints, her lover boy was inside. But, why was not he answering, she wondered as she entered to see her daughter still wrapped up and her papa not there. In the corner where her husband kept his rifle, there was nothing.

"Oh, my early bird, you are still asleep?" she called, as she collected some taro to peel. "You need some sunshine outside if you are feeling weak."

"Mama, you massage my hip," she gave a guttural cry in burning agony with a dull and exhausted voice, as she turned exposing blood and releasing the urine stench.

Murubita's taro slipped from her grip in disbelief. Her plot of roses was naked and had been touched by an invisible hand. Who was this thief? Who is this lover of Tobo'nu?

"Tobo'nu, tell me who is your lover here? In this jungle, who is the boy of yours with such a very big penis?" she asked. In her voice there was a tangle of anger and sorrow.

"Mama, your...your Tonepa did this ...."

"What! Tonepa ... Tonepa, you animal!" she gave out a hysterical scream that shook the entire valley. "Where is he, the pig?" She stood outside and called to the other camps: "Find Tonepa and kill him, he has just ruined my beloved virgin daughter."

The jungle came to life as people rushed and gathered around Murubita's camp. Tobo'nu's uncle stood up in tears and ordered: "My sister has called for me to do justice on behalf of my niece and I will not sleep until the dirt in my eyes and on the clan is executed and dumped at Lake Momau for the crocodiles to feast on." All agreed, and the men went off smelling every trail with their guns.

Inside the hut, sympathetic women nursed the injured young colleen, as Murubita wept. She gave out hysterical screams and rolled in the dust:

"Oi my daughter, my flower
I have ruined your beauty; your beloved papa is at the depths
Of the Buka Passage.
When will he come? When are you coming, our daughter has been
raped?

Oh my beloved,
Your father was killed by the New Guineans
And dumped in the sea
And now here you are in pain;
Oh, no papa to protect us."

She struggled to stand and hug her seated daughter but weakness got her down to the ground again and back to her desperate stuttering lamentations:

"Oh my daughter,
We have been defeated by a liar
Who had escaped but will be killed; will be gunned down
With the help of your father, Tonepa will be killed and dumped to
the crocodiles.
Oh my beauty,
My dirty cunt has betrayed you."

She stripped and threw away her laplap as she rolled and scooped dust onto her pubes:

"Oh my sunshine,
This vulva sold you to the dog that raped you.
Oh my clan,
These labia sold your pride, future and womb
To the parasite."

Her energies ebbed slowly like the sea receding at low tide and she slept in the dust. In the shock of defeat and agony she snored under the midday sun that was forcing itself through the overlapping jungle canopy to heal the wounds of the girl.

Ino - cassava cakes.
Kopero - water that runs through a supported bamboo pipe.

16
THE DAY UNANG WAS FLOODED

The morning was unusually dull. A once-a-year weather thing. A blanket of low creeping cloud – grey, wispy and soupy – swaddled up Unang hamlet. It was only just possible to see through it, though it was dark.

The Monday was ugly, cold and heart-chilling. Strangely forbidding for an aged one like Borukoi. But she was there!

In the semi-darkness, the lone silhouetted figure of *tete* Borukoi doddered out of her daughter Etai's *kavoro* with a burning faggot in her hand.

She re-entered her own *kavoro*. On their shared *mauko*, her granddaughter, Bari, was still muffled up in a blanket.

Borukoi squatted near the fireplace piling wood together. "*Era, tete*, still asleep?"

"Not really." She carelessly unwrapped; yawned and stretched. "Just, in some kind of doldrums. Nausea I think."

Bari crept out of bed with her left hand index finger pressed and rubbing against her hirsute head; in search of lice.

Her *tete* stared at her imploringly.

"It's that stinking smell of mud that is sickening. I feel like dying standing on the banks of the Kavarong ever since the *kakarari* started digging for precious stones upstream."

"What are those?" the old woman asked.

"Tete, don't ask me. But the men folk are naming a few like gold and copper and I don't know." She paused and grabbed her bamboo dibber. "To find these stones, the *kakarari* brought with them from England, machines that fly like birds; machines that dig like pigs; and some others, that behave like the crabs. Fear engulfed me at the first sight of them."

Silence lazily crept into the *kavoro*.

The crackling fire freed them from the harming spell of the arctic weather. It was burning furiously. Flames danced to the rhythm of the breeze as the pair watched in wonder. That sprouting comfort was immense.

Outside and beyond, the sun was now shining as trees lazily swayed and birds sang.

Gone was the fog that had blurred the morning. It had soared high and drifted north. Above, Panguna and over those dirty white men it settled - thick and heavy.

The pair had breakfast of boiled *ba'u and potu'raa* simmered in white coconut milk. Later, they sat chatting over a round of appetising betel nut.

"I think your sickness has ebbed?" Borukoi gave a smile exposing her reddish teeth and tongue; betel nut stain.

"*Masika'ra*, nice areca-nuts. Where did you get them?"

"Your mama, E'tai, gave them to me."

As they chatted thunder rumbled up in the north-east. The *kakarari* are trembling under the cat-and-dog rain Borukoi thought. Rascals, they deserve it, *mabai'nangka*!

She trailed her dibber behind outside. "Oi, the rain is edging at Pirurari. Kavarong will burst with befouled alluvial flood. We'll be submerged soon; this poor lawn of Unang."

"Why do you say that, *tete*?"

"Oi! Tete, look at that Kavarong Gorge, half of its space has being filled by silt. Continuous digging upstream then mud will soon, gormandize this whole valley."

"Masikara," Bari bent and grappled with the haft of an axe to chop firewood. "They have poisoned our eels and prawns, already, and still they aren't satisfied. Why did these Moroni and Guava people invite them here?"

"Money, for it our felled trees and fish are gone for good. These selfish mountain people have ruined our pride for good." Borukoi was tense.

Under the glare of the sun, Bari heaved her axe at the length of log as her beloved *tete* watched. Her agile and chocolate anatomy was moist with sweat; her skirt was wet in clammy patches.

The heat was so cruel; worsening every second.

Exhausted, she hurried to the shade of a slightly swaying mango tree. With both her palms clamped to her haunches she stood staring at the façade of her family house. A good rest was her goal. Or was it?

She was surprised by her approaching papa Dani's complexion – terrified, over exhausted and staid – she moved towards him. His body had been dragged in mud somewhere. Nowhere else but the dirty Kavarong it could be.

"Oi, Papa," Bari quizzed, with a frown, "where did the mud gloss you up, era?"

"I slipped off a rock, and ended in the filth at Bano'dua. Just prepare for the worst, daughter," dead beaten papa Dani snapped. His eyes were teary. "Mako'si and Poarunau have been submerged by flood. It's carrying with it large boles and quantities of debris. Terrific! It's likely to trounce this hamlet with flying colours."

"So, *tete* was a real harbinger!" she bolted off to see for herself.

To her eyes the river scene was hellish; absolutely, beyond her comprehension. The river overflowed its natural gorge. Before her, giant boles – a few with branches and leaves still attached – gestured farewell as they jostled their way to the coast. The naughty Kavarong wanted them in the distant Pacific Ocean.

A meandering line of mud and dirt marked the territory claimed so far. However, to her alarm, the line was approaching her. The river is hungry; she dashed off for home. Concerned and terrified.

"*Tete*! *Tete*." She shouted. "*Era*, the flood is coming for us. Papa said that we'll go to the higher ground. He just had a lucky escape from the hand of death himself."

"*Oi, noorang masi'kara eeng?*" Borukoi yawned and stepped out in the open. Why be bothered by the drizzle.

"Masi'kara, era." Bari popped out of the *kavoro* with her folded *karamani* in her hand, and a red blanket dangling on her right shoulder. She was ready for a run.

Borukoi stood befogged, her wrinkled face displaying affliction, uncertainty and a faraway look. Reluctantly, she ran her gaze over the whole hamlet – length to breath. If that flooding is real, then we are finished she thought. My pride shall be munched up by the bamboozled Kavarong.

This hamlet that she had girded herself in was obviously losing to the Kavarong's attrition. Under her very nose, fate was falling hard. Who will be accountable for this mundane loss? She felt really sick in the head. The Guava and Moroni people? The horizon, wherever it was, was dauntingly blurred.

She slouched through the banana garden to see the flooding. Her diligence had turned into a fiasco. The breadfruit she had planted many years ago was uprooted. It had landed on the ground messing up the bananas – her fruit bearing plants. Lord pity us!

Blocked by a boulder, the flood greedily began to excavate a new course off Unang hamlet, bifurcating in front of her aged eyes. Tears began to form in those eyes as she turned. She paced in a gait of defeat.

Her family - daughters, in-laws and grannies - watched her approaching in tears. In the background, the sickened river brawled; planted fruit trees jerked, heaved and then were submerged for eternity. The worst natural setback Unang had ever experienced was unfolding. Right behind flood water followed in like footprints on a trail.

"*Oi baka nuru'ka dovo*, these people have ruined our land, life and home." Her eyes were suffused with tears. "They've got no respect. Who do they think we are - animals?"

She threw her dibber against her *kavoro* in anger and sat

on the ground; hands raised in supplication. "The self-centred Guava and Moroni people must compensate us. *Orara nangka kongto.*" She hawked and spat into the air. "We hear them at the Barapingnang market talking about money. Money! Oh, hedonists! They are the white men's fart. *Parorii.*" Her sobbing was hysterical.

Bari stood patting her for comfort. *"Tete*, please stop your crying."

"No way, tete. Moan for your land. Shed your tears for the land; there was nothing but dignity and inspiration in your forefathers, which has now been despoiled before your very eyes by the white men and their sympathizers. They are plundering our heritage to feed their pockets of greed and dishonesty, my daughter. Weep without shame."

As she sat in her poetry of lamentation, her son Karepau arrived, his legs splotched knee-high with mud. Seeing the tear-stained and puffy eyes of his mama he gave a jocular jitter.

"So you are crying, mama. What, has Papa just died now?"

"Oh, Karepau, you and your jokes; get lost. See what now remains - or shall remain - that when I die you would eat and say, "Yes, this is what mama planted for me. The crass white man's Kavarong - not ours now - is taking it all away. A real iniquitous doing, you should say and tell your children, later on."

"You are talking the truth, Mama," Karepau commented in a wan voice, then helped her into a sitting position.

In the north, thunder fractiously rumbled as lightening zestfully flashed; the old signs of easing rain. Birds began singing after hours of idleness; obviously, laughing at the mud stained lawns of hamlet Unang. *Tete* Borukoi's *kavoro*, though, was untouched, but the mine stench infiltrated deep inside.

For the juvenile Bari, curiosity to explore the river side

obtruded.

"When the flood calms, I will …. "

"*Ena narapu'runang,* follow not your silly thoughts," Karepau interrupted "The sedimentation is too deep. Dangerous. Lethal. Don't let E'tai rename* herself 'Mud' when she loses you to the bog."

"*Masika'ra, era tete,*" Borukoi added. "Joy and life was always attached to this land, but that is not so now. We are now doomed."

At that, Bari calmly lifted a basket of sweet potato and marched, with a blackened pot in hand to the little brawling tributary that was Unang's cooking, bathing and drinking water that streams down the Onove brae from the west end of the hamlet.

Karepau was a lost child; his muscular body was intact but not his mind. "I…..I just don't know how these people will fix this mess." He shrugged hopelessly.

"*Oi-i nuring,*" his mama retorted. "You say, 'fix'?" Sorry they shall never happen. This is too much. Your educated uncle, Mirongko, told me that this mining is to finance Papua New Guinea's economy. Not us. No money for this rubbish, here."

"If, Mirongko said that, then, this 'rubbish' in our valley belongs to those little demagogues inside Moresby parliament. I will kill one of them if he enters this place during election time shouting his spiel."

"They are responsible," Borukoi said. "Corrupt idiots in faraway places; show offs!"

Karepau sat, bent with his chin resting on his palms. He was preoccupied.

"Era, mama," he wistfully suggested, "we need to relocate somewhere higher. Kavarongnau - the flat area occupied by your garden and that galip-nut shelter - seems suitable."

Borukoi stood up unsteadily. "Bari," she cried, tears forming in her eyes, make your way there; have these in-laws assist you in erecting shelters that will protect your little ones in the future. Not me, my days are over. No one will force me out of my Unang. My mother travelled here for me. Here, I belong." She went inside her *kavoro*.

Karepau shook his head. "Mama, are you serious?" he chuckled.

From inside the darkness of the *kavoro*: "Yes. Your grandmother cut my umbilical cord here, so, this is where I belong. You see, son, my skin has got no life. I wish I was one of those Africans you told me about that die by just willing themselves to death. I love that story when my beautiful valley is dancing on fire under this imperialistic looting."

"Mama," her son was calmly serious, "your thoughts are selfish and pointless. You are the family's spring of wisdom and inspiration; the light in the darkness. Without you, we are nothing. So, you need to relocate with us, rather than dreaming about early death. That's cowardice - dastardly talk."

In the darkness of the *kavoro*, silence; deathly silence, swirled. Minutes trickled by as she fumbled in her mind for solutions and explanations. And it finally dawned that her family needed her very much in this hostile and ill-mannered life.

"My family needs me, *masikara*," she loudly told herself. Her frail face was glittering with sweat in the flickering fire.

"*Tampara*, mama," complimented her son.

"But Karepau," she cried, "you must unearth the remains of your brother Deona from his grave and bring him to Kavarongnau if you really want me to move." She sobbed and continued. "Your brother was the victim of the selfish company and they won't give up; they are coming yet to destroy us."

"*Te tampa otong, ena.*" Karepau hugged his mama in tears of assurance. "I'll do that for you."

Tete - grandmother.
Mauko - large bed covering the whole half of a kitchen hut.

Era, tete - hey grand mother.
Kakarari - white man.
Kavoro - kitchen hut.
Ba'u and potu'raa - taro and fern.
Masika'ra - true.
Mabai'naagka - show offs.
Oi, noorang masi'kara eeng? - daughter, is it real?
Karamani - mai.
Oi baka kuru'ka dovo - oh, my children.
Orara nangka kongto - very bad people.
Parorii - spirit beings of the bush.
Ena nampu'runang - oh, my niece!
*A Kieta tradition of inheriting or changing a name of the place
where a loved one has died.
Oi-i nuring - oh my son.
Te tampa otong, ena - it is okay.

ABOUT THE AUTHOR

Leonard Fong Roka was born in 1979 in Arawa, then the capital of the North Solomons Province (Bougainville) in Papua New Guinea. He was the first born in the family and has a younger brother and three sisters.

His mother comes from Bougainville but his father's traditional home was Bali Island in West New Britain Province. His father never set his foot on his patrimonial land and grew up on Bougainville. He was killed by the Bougainville Revolutionary Army in 1993.

In 1994, just before the PNGDF and the Bougainville Resistance Forces attempted the recapture of the Panguna Mine, his courageous mother, after learning that schools in the PNGDF controlled areas were to be re-opened, led her family to Arawa.

Leonard had begun his schooling at the Piruana Village Tokples School outside Arawa in 1986. In 1987 he attended Peter Lahis Community School on the eastern edge of Arawa, where his father was the catechist for the Arawa Catholic Parish. He stayed there until 1989 when the Bougainville conflict intensified. In 1990 he and his younger brother were transferred to the centralized Kaperia Community School by their brother[1], the late Joseph Kabui, who was then Premier of the North Solomons.

The classes were halted midway by the PNG blockade on Bougainville. However, the 1994 ceasefire allowed him to re-enrol. He completed Arawa High School in 2000 and graduated from Hutjena Secondary School in 2002 and went to the University of Papua New Guinea in 2003. In 2004 financial difficulties forced him to abandon his studies.

He began writing poetry in 1997 while in Grade 7 at Arawa High School. After leaving university he took up numerous part-time jobs with various organisations in Bougainville. He also began writing short stories and started on a Bougainville Crisis autobiography project called *Brokenville*.

After 7 years out of the education system, he returned to university and is currently a student at Divine Word University in Madang.

---

[1] According to the Nasioi kinship system a person's mother's uncle is a brother.

www.ingramcontent.com/pod-product-compliance
Lightning Source LLC
Chambersburg PA
CBHW070749120626
46557CB00002B/515